THE FORCE

S0-AKQ-638

Follow the bestselling adventures for teen readers

STAR WARS:
YOUNG JEDI KNIGHTS

HEIRS OF THE FORCE

In the jungle outside the academy, the twins make a startling discovery—the remains of a crashed TIE fighter. The original pilot, an Imperial trooper, has been living wild in the jungles since his crash. Waiting for a chance to return to duty . . .

SHADOW ACADEMY

Thanks to the Dark Jedi Brakiss—Luke Skywalker's former student—the dark side of the Force has a new training ground. The Shadow Academy!

THE LOST ONES

Jacen and Jaina could lose an old and dear friend! Zekk is wild and free in the underground mazes of Coruscant . . . and the perfect candidate for the Shadow Academy!

And now, the Young Jedi Knights' most exciting adventure:

LIGHTSABERS

This book also contains a special sneak preview of the next *Star Wars: Young Jedi Knights* adventure:

DARKEST KNIGHT

ABOUT THE AUTHORS

KEVIN J. ANDERSON and his wife, **REBECCA MOESTA**, have been involved in many STAR WARS projects. Together, they are writing the eleven volumes of the YOUNG JEDI KNIGHTS saga for young adults, as well as creating the JUNIOR JEDI KNIGHTS series for younger readers. They are also writing pop-up books showcasing the Cantina scene and the Jabba's Palace scene.

Kevin J. Anderson is also the author of the STAR WARS: JEDI ACADEMY trilogy, the novel *Darksaber*, and the comic series THE SITH WAR for Dark Horse comics. His young adult fantasy novel, *Born of Elven Blood*, written with John Betancourt, was published in 1995 by Atheneum. He has edited several STAR WARS anthologies, including *Tales From the Mos Eisley Cantina,* in which Rebecca Moesta has a story, and *Tales from Jabba's Palace.*

STAR WARS

YOUNG JEDI KNIGHTS

LIGHTSABERS

KEVIN J. ANDERSON
and REBECCA MOESTA

BERKLEY JAM BOOKS, NEW YORK

STAR WARS: YOUNG JEDI KNIGHTS:
LIGHTSABERS

A Berkley Jam Book / published by arrangement with
Lucasfilm Ltd.

PRINTING HISTORY
Boulevard edition / March 1996
Berkley Jam edition / March 1999

All rights reserved.
®, ™ & Copyright © 1996 by Lucasfilm Ltd.
Material excerpted from DARKEST KNIGHT
copyright © 1996 by Lucasfilm Ltd.
This book may not be reproduced in whole or in part,
by mimeograph or any other means, without permission.
For information address: The Berkley Publishing Group,
a member of Penguin Putnam Inc.,
375 Hudson Street, New York, New York 10014.

The Penguin Putnam Inc. World Wide Web site address is
http://www.penguinputnam.com

ISBN: 0-425-16951-0

BERKLEY JAM BOOKS®
Berkley Jam Books are published by The Berkley Publishing Group,
a member of Penguin Putnam Inc.,
375 Hudson Street, New York, New York 10014.
BERKLEY JAM and its logo
are trademarks belonging to Berkley Publishing Corporation.

PRINTED IN THE UNITED STATES OF AMERICA

10 9 8 7

To Jonathan MacGregor Cowan,
whose love, intelligence, imagination, sense of humor,
and sense of wonder constantly inspire us—and challenge us.

acknowledgments

We would like to thank Lillie E. Mitchell for her spectacular typing and her love of the books, Dave Wolverton for his input on the Hapes Cluster, Lucy Wilson and Sue Rostoni at Lucasfilm for their constructive comments and their vision, Ginjer Buchanan and Lou Aronica at Berkley/ Boulevard for their wholehearted support and encouragement, and Skip and Cheryl Shayotovich for being some of our most faithful cheerleaders.

DAYBREAK AT LAST spilled across the treetops on Yavin 4, where Luke Skywalker, Jedi Master, listened to the stirring, rustling sounds of the awakening jungle. The looming stone blocks of the ancient temple had absorbed the deep night's chill, and now glistened with dew.

As the morning brightened, he wished his spirits could lift as easily.

Cool and stiff, Luke had been atop the Great Temple for a long time already, sitting patiently in the primeval darkness and thinking. He had used Jedi relaxation techniques to dispense with sleep; in fact, he had not rested thoroughly for some time, so great was his concern over the growing Imperial threat to the New Republic.

Jungle birds cried out and took wing, searching for a breakfast of flying insects. The enormous gas giant Yavin hung overhead, luminous with reflected light, but Luke stared beyond it with his imagination, envisioning all of the galaxy's dark and secret corners where the Second Imperium might lie hidden. . . .

Finally Luke stood and stretched. It was time for his morning exercises. Perhaps the exertion would help him think more clearly, get his heart beating harder, tune his reflexes.

At the top of the pyramid, he went to the sheer edge of the enormous, vine-covered blocks that formed the sides of the towering temple. It was a long drop to the next level, where the ziggurat widened toward its base. Each squared-off set of blocks displayed decorative etchings and crenellations, carved into the stone thousands of years earlier during the building of the ancient structure, weathered by scorching attack and passing time. The dense jungle encroached at the rear of the temple pyramid, embellishing the massive stones with thick vines and overspreading Massassi tree branches.

Luke paused for a moment at the edge, took a deep breath, and closed his eyes to center his concentration. Then he leaped out into space.

He felt himself falling and rotated in midair, executing a backward somersault that brought him into position, feet down, just in time to see the cracked old stones rushing up at him. Using the Force to slow himself just enough for a hard landing, he rebounded and pushed off toward the nearest vine. Allowing himself a brief laugh of exhilaration, Luke snagged the rough jungle creeper and swung up onto the lichen-flaked branch of a Massassi tree. He landed smoothly and ran along the branch without pausing. Next he jumped across a gap in the jungle canopy and grabbed a small branch overhead, hauling himself higher, climbing, running.

Each day Luke challenged himself, finding more difficult routines in order to continue honing his skills. Even during times of peace, a Jedi Knight could never allow himself to relax and grow weak.

But these were not quiet times, and Luke Skywalker had plenty of challenges to face.

Years ago, a student named Brakiss had been planted in Luke's academy as an Imperial spy to learn the ways of the Jedi and twist them to evil uses. Luke had seen through the disguise, however, and had tried unsuccessfully to turn Brakiss to the light side. After the dark trainee had fled, Luke had not heard from Brakiss again—until recently, when Jacen, Jaina, and the young Wookiee Lowbacca had been kidnapped. Brakiss had teamed up with one of the evil new Nightsisters—Tamith Kai—to form a Shadow Academy for training Dark Jedi in the service of the Empire.

Panting from his workout, Luke continued to climb through the trees, startling a nest of ravenous stintarils. The rodents turned on him, flashing bright teeth, but when he nudged their attack instincts in a new direction, they forgot their intended target and scattered through the leafy branches.

He swung himself up and finally reached the jungle canopy. Sunshine burst upon him as he pushed his head above the leafy treetops. Humid air filled his burning lungs, and he blinked again in the morning light. The lush world around him seemed very bright after the filtered dimness of the thick underlevels. Looking back toward the stepped pyramid of the Great Temple that housed his Jedi students, Luke considered both the new group of fighters he had brought here to help protect the New Republic and the trainees at the Shadow Academy. . . .

In the past few months, the Shadow Academy had begun recruiting candidates among the disadvantaged young men and women of Coruscant, taking these "lost ones" to serve the Second Imperium. One of these had been the teenager named Zekk, a dark-haired, green-eyed scamp who had been a good friend to the twins, especially Jaina. In addition, the TIE pilot Qorl—who had spent over two decades hiding on Yavin 4 after the first Death Star was destroyed—had led a raid to steal hyperdrive cores and turbolaser batteries from an incoming New Republic supply ship.

All this and more had led Luke Skywalker to the conclusion that the Shadow Academy was gearing up for a major battle against the New Republic.

Since the death of Emperor Palpatine, there had been many warlords and leaders who had attempted to rekindle the Imperial way—but Luke sensed through the Force that this new leader was something more evil than just another pretender. . . .

Bright sunlight fell across Luke, warming his hands. Brilliantly colored insects flitted about, buzzing in the new day. He shifted against the rough branches and drew a deep breath of the fresh air, catching mingled scents from the lush jungle all around him.

The Shadow Academy was still out there, still training Dark Jedi. Luke hated to rush his training of those who studied the ways of the light side—but circumstances forced him to attempt to bring out powerful defenders faster than the Shadow Academy could create new enemies. A fight was brewing, and they had to be prepared.

Luke grabbed a loose vine and let himself drop, drop, *drop* until, landing with a jarring thump against a wide Massassi tree branch, he set off, running at top speed back to the academy.

The workout had awakened him fully, and now he was ready for action.

It was time for another gathering of students at the Jedi academy—and Jacen Solo knew that meant his uncle, Luke Skywalker, had something important to say.

Life at the academy was not a constant series of lectures and classes, as he had experienced during tutoring sessions back on Coruscant. The Jedi academy was designed primarily for independent study in a place where Force-sensitive individuals could delve into their minds, test their abilities, and work at their own pace.

Each potential Jedi Knight had a range of skills. Jacen himself had a knack for understanding animals, calling them to him, and knowing their thoughts and feelings. His sister Jaina, on the other hand, had a genius for mechanical things and electronic circuits, and possessed engineering intuition.

Lowbacca, their Wookiee friend, had an eerie rapport with computers, which allowed him to decipher and program complex electronic circuits. Their athletic friend Tenel Ka was physically strong and self-trained, but she usually avoided relying on the Force as the easiest solution to a problem. Tenel Ka depended on her own wits and strength first.

In his quarters Jacen's exotic pets rustled in their cages along the stone wall. He hurried to feed them and then ran his fingers through his unruly brown curls to remove any stray bits of moss or fodder he might have picked up from the cages. He poked his head into his twin sister Jaina's chambers as she, too, prepared for the big meeting. She quickly combed her straight brown hair and scrubbed her face clean so that her skin looked pink and fresh.

"Any idea what Uncle Luke's going to talk about?" she asked, drying drips of water from her chin and nose.

"I was hoping you'd know," Jacen said.

One of the other young Jedi trainees, Raynar, emerged from his room dressed in garishly colored robes with an eye-popping display of intense primary blues, yellows, and reds. He seemed terribly flustered as he brushed his hands down the fabric of his robe, let out a sigh of dismay, and ducked back into his rooms.

"Bet the meeting has something to do with that trip Uncle Luke just took to Coruscant," Jaina said. Jacen remembered that their uncle had recently flown off in the *Shadow Chaser*—a sleek ship they had appropriated from the Shadow Academy in order to make good their escape—to discuss the threat of the Second Imperium with Chief of State Leia Organa Solo, Luke's sister and the twins' mother.

"Only one way to find out," Jacen said. "Most of the other students should be in the grand audience chamber already."

"Well then, what are we waiting for?" Jaina said, and took off with her brother at a brisk clip down the corridor.

Behind them, Raynar emerged from his quarters again, looking much more satisfied now that he had managed to find a robe that was, if anything, even more dazzlingly bright than the first one—enough to cause tension headaches in anyone who looked too long. Raynar cinched the robe around his waist with a green and orange patterned sash, then bustled after Jacen and Jaina.

When they stepped out of the turbolift into the grand audience chamber, the twins looked at the restless crowd of human and alien students, some with two arms and two legs, others with many times that. Some had fur, others had feathers, scales, or slick damp skin . . . but all had a talent for the Force, the potential—if they trained and studied diligently—to eventually become members of a new order of Jedi Knights that was growing stronger with each passing year.

Over the background chatter they heard a resounding Wookiee bellow, and Jacen pointed. "There's Lowie! He's with Tenel Ka already."

They hurried down the central aisle, passing other students and slipping between rows of stone benches to reach their two friends. Jaina held back and waited while her brother took a seat next to Tenel Ka, as he always did.

Jacen wondered if his twin sister had noticed how much he liked being with Tenel Ka, how he always chose a place beside the young warrior girl. Then he realized that Jaina would never miss anything of that sort—but he didn't really care.

Tenel Ka didn't seem to object to Jacen spending

his time next to her. The two of them were an odd mix. Jacen always wore an impish grin and enjoyed joking around. Ever since they had met, one of his main goals had been to make Tenel Ka laugh by telling her silly jokes. But despite his best efforts, the strong girl with reddish-gold hair remained serious, almost grim, though he knew she was intelligent, quick to act, and profoundly loyal.

"Greetings, Jacen," Tenel Ka said.

"How are you doing, Tenel Ka? Hey, I've got another joke for you."

Lowbacca groaned, and Jacen shot him a wounded look.

"There is no time," Tenel Ka said, pointing toward the speaker's platform. "Master Skywalker is about to address us."

Indeed, Luke had come out onto the stage and stood in his Jedi robe. His face deeply serious, he folded his hands in front of him, and the audience quickly grew quiet.

"A time of great darkness is upon us," Master Skywalker said. The silence grew even deeper. Jacen sat straight and looked around in alarm.

"Not only does the Empire continue its struggles to reclaim the galaxy, but this time it is using the Force in an unprecedented manner. With its Shadow Academy, the leaders of the Second Imperium are creating their own army of dark side Force-wielders. And *we*, my friends, are the only ones who can stand against it." He paused as that news sank in. Jacen swallowed hard.

"Though the Emperor has been dead for nineteen years, still the New Republic struggles to bring the worlds of the galaxy into an alliance. Palpatine did not take so long to squeeze his iron fist around star systems—but the New Republic is a different kind of government. We aren't willing to use the Emperor's tactics. The Chief of State will not send armed fleets to crush planets into submission or execute dissidents. Unfortunately, though, because we use peaceful democratic means, we are more vulnerable to a threat like the Empire."

Jacen felt warm inside at the mention of his mother and what she was doing with the New Republic.

"In days long past," Luke said, walking from side to side on the stage so that he seemed to be talking to each one of them in turn, "a Jedi Master spent years looking for a single student to teach and guide along the path of the Jedi." Luke's voice became graver. "Now, though, our need is too great for such caution. The Empire nearly succeeded in obliterating the Jedi Knights of old, and we don't have the luxury of such patience. Instead, I'm going to have to ask you to learn a little faster, to grow strong a little sooner. I must accelerate your training, *because the New Republic needs more Jedi Knights*."

From one of the front rows, where he always sat,

Raynar spoke up. Jacen had to blink to clear the spots of bright color from his vision when the sandy-haired boy raised his hand. "We're ready, Master Skywalker! We're all willing to fight for you."

Luke looked intently at the boy who had interrupted him. "I'm not asking you to fight for *me*, Raynar," Luke said in a calm voice. "I need your help to fight *for* the New Republic, and *against* the evil ways we thought were behind us. Not for any one person."

The students stirred. Their minds churned with a determination they didn't know how to direct.

Master Skywalker continued to pace. "Each of you must work individually to stretch your abilities. I'll help as I can. I want to meet with you in small groups to plan strategy, discuss ways to help each other. We must be strong, because I believe with all my heart that we face dark times ahead."

Down in the echoing hangar bay beneath the temple, Jacen crouched in a cool corner, extending his mind into a crack between blocks where he sensed a rare red and green stinger lizard. He sent a tendril of thought to it, imaginary enticements of food—dismissing reptilian concerns of danger. Jacen very much wanted to add the lizard to his collection of unusual pets.

Lowbacca and Jaina tinkered with Lowie's T-23

skyhopper, the flying craft that his uncle Chewbacca had given him when he'd brought the young Wookiee to the Jedi academy. Jacen knew his sister was a bit jealous of Lowie for having his own flying machine. In fact, that had been one of the reasons Jaina had so badly wanted to repair the crashed TIE fighter they'd found out in the jungle.

Tenel Ka stood outside the upraised horizontal door of the hangar bay. She held a forked wooden spear that she used for target practice, throwing it with exceptional skill toward a tiny mark on the landing pad. The teenaged warrior could strike her target with either hand. She stared at her goal with cool, granite-gray eyes, focused her concentration, and then let the sharpened stick fly.

Tenel Ka could have nudged the spear with the Force, guiding it where she wished it to go—but Jacen knew from long experience that she would probably tackle him to the ground if he dared suggest such a thing. Tenel Ka had gained her physical skill through faithful practice and was reluctant to use the Force in a way that she considered to be cheating. She was very proud of her skills.

In the rear of the hangar bay, the turbolift hummed. Master Luke Skywalker emerged and looked around. Jacen gave up his designs on the stinger lizard and stood. His knees cracked, and his ankles were sore, which made him realize how long he had crouched motionless. "Hi, Uncle Luke," he said.

Tenel Ka threw her spear one last time, then retrieved it and turned to meet Luke. She and the Jedi Master had shared a special bond from the time the two of them had spent together searching for the kidnapped twins and Lowie and rescuing them from the Shadow Academy . . . though Jacen sensed that Tenel Ka and Uncle Luke shared other secrets as well.

"Greetings, Master Skywalker," Tenel Ka said.

The tinny voice of Em Teedee, the miniaturized translator droid hanging from a clip on Lowbacca's belt, chimed out, "Master Lowbacca, we have a guest. If you're quite finished fussing with those controls, I believe Master Skywalker wishes to converse with you."

Lowie grunted and raised his shaggy head, scratching the remarkable black streak of fur that rose over one eyebrow and curved down his back.

Jaina scrambled up beside him. "What is it? Oh, hi, Uncle Luke."

"I'm glad you're all here," Luke said. "I wanted to discuss your training. You four have been in closer contact with the Second Imperium than my other students, so you know the danger better than they do. You also all have extraordinarily strong Jedi potential, and I think perhaps you're ready for a greater challenge than the others."

"Like what?" Jacen asked eagerly.

"Like taking the next step toward becoming full Jedi Knights," Luke said.

Jacen's mind spun, trying to figure out what his uncle meant, but Jaina exclaimed, "You want us to build our own lightsabers, don't you?"

"Yes," Luke nodded. "I normally wouldn't suggest this so early, especially for such young students. But I think we're in for a battle so difficult that I want you to be prepared to use every weapon at your disposal."

Jacen felt a surge of delight, followed by sudden uneasiness. Not long ago he had desperately wanted his own lightsaber, but he had been forced to train with one at the Shadow Academy . . . and he and his sister had come close to killing each other in a deceptive test. "But, Uncle Luke, I thought you said it was too dangerous for us."

Luke nodded soberly. "It *is* dangerous. As I recall, I once caught you playing with my weapon because you wanted one so much—but I think you've learned an important lesson since then about taking lightsabers seriously."

Jacen agreed. "Yeah, I don't think I'll ever again think of a lightsaber as a toy."

Luke smiled back at him. "Good. That's an important start," he said. "These weapons are not playthings. A lightsaber is a dangerous and destructive instrument, a powerful blade that can strike down an opponent—or a friend, if you're not careful."

"We'll be careful, Uncle Luke," Jaina assured him with an earnest nod.

Luke still seemed skeptical. "This isn't a reward. It's an obligation, a difficult new set of lessons for you. Perhaps the work involved in building your own lightsaber will teach you to respect it as a tool, as you learn how the Jedi created their own personal weapons, each with its special characteristics."

"Always wanted to know how a lightsaber worked. Can I take yours apart, Uncle Luke?" Jaina asked, her brandy-brown eyes pleading.

Now Luke let a smile cross his face. "I don't think so, Jaina—but you'll learn about them soon enough." He looked at the four young Jedi Knights. "I want you to begin without delay."

2

JAINA PAID ATTENTION to her uncle Luke's words with only half a mind, the rest of her concentration focusing on the problem of where to get the precious components for building her very own lightsaber.

She and her brother, along with Lowie and Tenel Ka, were in one of the upper solariums in the Great Temple, a room made of polished marble slabs inset with semiprecious stones. Bright light streamed through tall, narrow windows that had been chiseled into the stone blocks by ancient Massassi tribesmen.

Luke Skywalker sat nearby on a deep window ledge, uncharacteristically relaxed and boyish. He enjoyed being with a small group of trainees, especially his niece and nephew and their friends, talking about things that interested him.

"You may have heard about Jedi Masters during the Clone Wars who were able to fashion light-sabers in only a day or two, using whatever raw materials were at hand," Luke said. "But don't get the idea that your weapon is a quick little project to be slapped together. Ideally, a Jedi took many months to construct a single perfect weapon that he or she would keep and use for a lifetime. Once you build it, the lightsaber will become your constant companion, your tool, and a ready means of defense."

He stood up from his seat on the window ledge. "The components are fairly simple. Every lightsaber has a standard power source, the same type used in small blasters, even in glowpanels. They last a long time, though, because Jedi should rarely use their lightsabers."

"Got some of those power sources in my room," Jaina said. "Spare parts, you know."

"One of the other crucial pieces," Luke continued, "is a focusing crystal. The most powerful and sought-after gems are rare kaiburr crystals. However, though lightsabers are powerful weapons, their design is so flexible that practically any kind of crystal can be used. And, since I don't happen to have a stash of kaiburr crystals"—he smiled—"you'll have to make do with something else, of your own choosing."

Luke held out the handle of his own lightsaber, sliding his palm over the smooth grip, then igniting it with a startling snap-hiss. The brilliant yellow-green blade drowned out even the bright sunlight in the room.

"This is not my first lightsaber." Luke drew it

back and forth through the empty air so that its hum changed frequency. "Note the color of its blade. I lost my first lightsaber years ago . . . my father's lightsaber." He swallowed and seemed to struggle against a dark memory from his past. Jaina knew the story of how Luke had lost his other lightsaber during a duel with Darth Vader on Cloud City. In that terrible fight Luke Skywalker had lost not only his lightsaber, but his hand as well.

"My first weapon had a pale blue beam. The colors vary, according to the frequencies of the crystals used. Darth Vader's lightsaber"—he drew a deep breath—"*my father's* lightsaber was a deep scarlet."

Jaina nodded solemnly. She remembered fighting Vader's holographic image on the Shadow Academy—though it had actually been her own brother Jacen in disguise. Her lightsaber experiences had not been pleasant on the Imperial station . . . and now her feelings about the energy blades were even more confused. Her friend Zekk had also been taken by Brakiss and the Second Imperium. Jaina knew she would have to fight to get him back.

Luke continued, "One of my students, Cilghal, a Calamarian like Admiral Ackbar, made her lightsaber with smooth curves and protrusions, as if the handle had been grown from metallic coral. Inside, she used a rare ultima-pearl, one of the treasures found in the seabeds of her watery planet.

"My first true failure as a teacher was another student named Gantoris. He built his lightsaber in only a few intense days, following instructions given to him by the evil spirit of Exar Kun. Gantoris thought he was ready, and my mistake was not seeing what he was up to.

"You, my young Jedi Knights, must be different. I can't wait any longer to train you. You must learn how to build your lightsabers—and how to use them—in the right way. The galaxy has changed, and you must meet the challenge. A true Jedi is forced to adapt or be destroyed."

Tenel Ka spoke up. "Where will we find these crystals to build our weapons, Master Skywalker?" she asked. "Are they lying on the ground?"

Luke smiled. "Perhaps. Or it's possible they could be scavenged from old equipment left here from when this place was a Rebel base. Or maybe you already have resources you haven't yet realized." He shot a quick look at Jacen, but Jaina couldn't decipher what the glance meant.

"I'd like you to start on your lightsabers immediately." Luke switched off his throbbing weapon and looked down at its handle. "But I hope you'll need to use your weapons only rarely . . . if ever."

A few days later, Jaina sat hunched over her worktable inside her quarters. She had strung up extra glowpanels to allow her sufficient illumination to work through the night. Dozens of tools and pieces of equipment lay on the tabletop, arranged in a careful order so that she knew where every component, every wire and circuit might be found.

After Jaina had given each of her friends an appropriate power source to build their own light-sabers, the young Jedi Knights had split up to search for the precious crystals and other components that would make their new weapons function. Jaina, though, wanted to make the lightsaber particularly *hers*, a symbolic extension of her unique personality. She would make it from scratch in a way that the others would never attempt. She smiled at her own ingenuity.

Dark smoke rose from the portable furnace she had brought in, and she blinked to clear the chemical fumes from her eyes as she bent over it. Carefully, she added the next batch of powdered elements in the precise mixture her datapad suggested. She drew on her Force powers, amplifying her vision to observe the chemicals interacting, to watch them bond into a tight, organized lattice.

The precisely pure crystals began to grow. . . .

She adjusted the temperature, watching intently, though the process of crystalline growth took hours. She focused her mind on shaping the facets as they emerged from the molten mixture in the furnace, making the planes tilt at appropriate angles. The growing crystals gobbled up and stored the extra energy pumped into the mixture by the furnace.

Finally, by morning, her eyes bloodshot and gritty from lack of sleep, Jaina shut down the system. She let the furnace cool until she could reach in and take out her beautiful, sparkling crystals.

They were a rich purplish blue, shimmering with inner energy. They had formed perfectly, as she had expected, guided by her own mental skills. She held them in her palm and smiled. Now for the next step.

The tip of Jacen's tongue stuck out between his lips as he focused with unaccustomed concentration on the mechanical task at hand. It had already taken him a week to get this far.

He wanted to rush through the project, jam the components into place, connect the power, and turn on his lightsaber—his *own* lightsaber—but he took Uncle Luke's words seriously. This was a weapon he would use for the rest of his life, the weapon of a Jedi. A few weeks didn't seem so long to invest in creating it.

Much as it went against his nature to do so, Jacen forced himself to be meticulous and patient, knowing that he had to make sure everything fit together *just so* in the precise configuration required.

He had the power source Jaina had given him, and it was easy to find pieces of metal in the right shape and size to form the casing. He used Jaina's tools to cut the pieces into interlocking configurations and file down the rough edges. After a few days of doing that, he installed the power source, connecting all the leads. Then he added the control buttons.

Jaina could have whipped the casing together in just a few minutes, but it took him days to gather all the parts. Now, even though his scavenger hunt was over, it still seemed to take forever to assemble the thing.

Jacen would rather have been outside hunting for more specimens to add to his menagerie—or better yet, playing with the ones that cheerfully bounced about in their cages, often housed mere centimeters from other creatures that would gladly have had them for breakfast.

He heard the crystal snake rustling in its repaired cage, and then one of the reptile birds began to chirrup—but Jacen steeled himself, focusing on the project at hand. The lightsaber was almost finished, almost finished! He would be the first to complete his, and Master Luke would be very proud.

With the handle mostly assembled, he wrapped special grip-textured bindings around it so that he could hold and wield the blade with the gentle ease of a Jedi swordsman. Now Jacen was ready to install the powerful crystal.

He went to the personal locker box where he kept his valuable possessions and withdrew a small, glittering object—a Corusca gem. He had snared

the gem during a mining demonstration at Lando
Calrissian's GemDiver Station, and had later used it
to cut himself free from his locked quarters in the
Shadow Academy. He had offered the jewel to his
mother as a special gift—but she had persuaded
Jacen to keep the gem, to find a special use for it.

And what could be more special than using it in
his own lightsaber?

Lowbacca prowled through the clutter in the
former Rebel control room, left over from when
the Great Temple had been used as a base in the
struggle against the Empire. The soldiers had left
most of their old equipment here when they fled the
small jungle moon. In the years since, most of the
machinery and computers had bccn gutted for other
purposes, since Luke Skywalker's Jedi academy did
not rely heavily on gadgets and technology. Although Jaina had already scavenged these rooms,
Lowie knew that a great deal of equipment still
remained to be picked through.

Poking his snout into shadowy corners, the Wookiee snuffled and rumbled thoughtfully to himself. He
liftcd metal coverings to look around, rummaging
through wires and circuit boards, taking apart flat-
screen displays.

"Master Lowbacca, I simply cannot imagine
what you think you're accomplishing," Em Teedee
said from the clip at his waist. "You've been

prodding around here for hours, and you've found nothing."

Lowie let out a short growl.

"Well, really! No, I *don't* believe you can sniff them out with your nose. What an absurd notion! How could anyone possibly sniff out a crystal?" Em Teedee's temper seemed to be getting short and Lowie wondered if perhaps the little translating droid's batteries were running low.

"Anyway, I doubt you'll ever locate any kind of crystal in here. I'm sure the entire control room was thoroughly ransacked years ago."

Lowie barked a comment as he continued his search.

"Quite the contrary," Em Teedee said. "I am not a pessimist—I'm simply being realistic. I don't know why Master Skywalker should expect everyone to simply *find* appropriate crystals here or there. What if one of you created an inferior lightsaber? What good would that do? I daresay it's a possibility. I really think you should give up the search."

With a sudden bellow of triumph, Lowie reached into the cluttered interior of a small, high-resolution projection system and withdrew two glittering components: a flat focusing lens and a spherical enhancement jewel. The items had been used in the high-res display, and Lowie knew instinctively that they could be applied to the same general purpose inside his new lightsaber.

With great delight, he held them in his long hairy fingers in front of Em Teedee's optical sensors. He growled with pleasure, and a hint of smugness.

Em Teedee replied with some degree of petulance, "Well, of course I could be wrong."

3

DAYBREAK FOUND TENEL Ka atop the Great Temple limbering up in preparation for her new exercise routine. After tying back her wavy red-gold hair with a few simple braids, she stretched each muscle slowly, deliberately, efficiently. Her lizard-skin bodysuit was even more abbreviated than her usual reptilian armor, so as not to restrict her movement. The sparkling blue scales rippled with every flexing of her muscles.

Standing barefoot on the ancient weathered stone of the temple, Tenel Ka reached toward the sky, stretching first with one arm, then the other. She felt her body begin to loosen up, as the jungle around her blossomed with the scents and sounds of the dawning day. A light breeze stirred the leaves, and Tenel Ka took in deep breaths, letting her mind focus on what she needed to do. She would make her new routine as rigorous as the calisthenics Master Skywalker himself performed each morning.

She had been surprised by her reaction to the Jedi

teacher's instruction for them to build their own lightsabers. Despite her fierce pride at knowing she would soon begin earnest training for real battles, Tenel Ka had resented the implication that she would somehow be judged on the basis of the *weapon* with which she would fight.

Earlier, she had scaled the Great Temple using nothing more than her grappling hook, her fibercord, and her own muscles. Wasn't the warrior who wielded the weapon much more important than the weapon itself? she asked herself. Even holding a simple stick instead of a dazzling lightsaber, Tenel Ka was capable of defeating an enemy.

When she felt truly limbered up, Tenel Ka hefted the meter-long wooden staff she had carried to the top of the temple. For half an hour she practiced throwing the stick into the air and catching it, alternating between her left hand and her right, first with eyes open, then closed. Next, she practiced twirling the wooden rod over her head and jumping over it as she swung it beneath her feet.

Perspiration glistened on Tenel Ka's neck and forehead, and was trickling down her spine by the time she moved on to the next challenge. Finally, once Tenel Ka was satisfied that her reflexes were as finely tuned as she could wish, she grasped one end of the staff with both hands as if it were a lightsaber and began sword drills.

After an hour of that, Tenel Ka was ready for

more exacting physical activity. Taking a deep breath, she sprinted down the steep outer stairs of the pyramid to ground level and began her ten-kilometer run for the day.

The breeze felt cool against her face as she ran. Glancing down at herself, she assessed her lean muscular arms and long sturdy legs, reveling in the unrestricted motion and complete control. She sped up, pleased to note that her muscles were more than equal to the demands she made on them.

Yes, she decided, the *warrior* was what mattered, not the weapon.

After her fifth day of intensive drilling to hone her skills as sharp as any weapon, Tenel Ka felt ready to begin fashioning the handle of her personal lightsaber. Still glowing with perspiration from her morning workout, she decided to swim in the warm jungle river while she considered her next task.

She thought of the many materials available for her lightsaber handle, as she stripped off her exercise suit and dove with easy confidence into the swift current. Tenel Ka was a strong swimmer, trained on both Hapes and Dathomir, at the insistence of both grandmothers. It was one of the few times she could remember that her parents' mothers had ever agreed on anything.

Augwynne Djo, mother of Teneniel Djo, Tenel Ka's mother, had taught her to swim, saying that the strongest hunters and warriors were those who could not be stopped by a mere lake or river. Ta'a Chume, on the other hand, matriarch of the Royal House of Hapes and mother of Tenel Ka's father, Prince Isolder, had taught swimming as a defense against assassins or kidnappers. In fact, her grandmother had once escaped an attempt on her life by jumping from a wavespeeder into a lake and swimming for shore underwater, so that the would-be assassins assumed she had drowned.

Tenel Ka surfaced from the river, drew a deep lungful of air, and struck out upstream against the current. It was difficult swimming, but she used the added strength she had gained in her recent lightsaber training . . . which brought her back to the task at hand.

She supposed she could fashion her lightsaber handle from a piece of metal pipe, or even carve one from hardwood, since a lightsaber gave off little heat. But somehow those did not seem right for her.

Tenel Ka propelled herself forward with long smooth strokes, keeping a steady rhythm. Left. Right. Left. Right.

Stone would be too difficult to shape, and too heavy for her purposes. Tenel Ka needed something that would suit the *image* of a warrior from Dathomir. She pictured Augwynne Djo's proud form clad in reptile skin, a ceremonial helm on her head, riding a domesticated rancor. The taming of these ferocious beasts was an appropriate symbol of the courage of her rugged people, since the huge beasts were powerful and their sharp claws deadly.

Tenel Ka allowed herself to sink below the surface of the river and changed to a new stroke, recalling that she had kept two teeth from her grandmother's favorite rancor when it had died a few years ago. They were not the rancor's largest teeth by far, but each *was* the perfect size and shape to be a lightsaber handle. . . .

A week later, Tenel Ka studied her handiwork with justifiable pride and etched another deep groove into the pattern she had carved on her rancor tooth.

Lowie, sitting ahead of her in the tiny cockpit of the T-23 skyhopper, turned and roared a question at her. She waited for a moment for Em Teedee's translation. "Master Lowbacca wishes to inquire whether you have any preference as to the volcano in which you hope to search for crystals."

Tenel Ka glanced out at the rich green jungle canopy rushing beneath them. "You may choose," she said.

Lowbacca gave a short bark. "It makes little difference to Master Lowbacca," Em Teedee told her. "He has already assembled the components he intends to use for his lightsaber. The primary construction on his instrument is complete, and he has only to tune it now."

Tenel Ka blinked in surprise, not only at the length of Em Teedee's translation after Lowbacca's short reply, but also at the thought that Lowbacca—and perhaps Jacen or Jaina—was so far ahead of her. Well then, she would have to make her search quickly and assemble her lightsaber without delay.

"The closest volcano," she said, reaching forward and pointing. "There." Then, gruffly, because she felt foolish for having asked Lowbacca to take her out on this errand, she said, "I apologize. I would not have troubled you with my request had I known your lightsaber was almost complete."

The Wookiee growled and dismissed this with a motion of one ginger-furred hand. "Master Lowbacca wishes to assure you that you have not inconvenienced him in the slightest," Em Teedee supplied. "It has been many days since he enjoyed solitude and meditation out in the jungle, and he delights in the opportunity to assist you in this manner."

The Wookiee snorted and gave the little translator droid a flick with one finger. "Oh—that is to say," Em Teedee amended, "it was Master Lowbacca's intention to take a break anyway, and he's pleased he could help."

The young Wookiee sniffed loudly, but accepted this translation. He brought the T-23 skyhopper down on a patch of hard-packed volcanic sand between the jungle's edge and the base of a small volcano. After Lowbacca woofed a few words, Em Teedee said, "When you have completed your search, successful or not, simply return here to the T-23. Master Lowbacca and I will watch for you from the treetops."

Tenel Ka nodded curtly. "Understood. Thank you." Without further ado, she turned and hurried up the slope toward the volcano.

Though none of the volcanoes near the Jedi academy had erupted in quite some time, tendrils of white steam still curled from this one's peak. Skirting the sharp black rocks on the perimeter, Tenel Ka soon found a gaping lava tube leading in toward the core of the volcano, as she had hoped.

A pungent sulfurous odor filled the warm tunnel. Tenel Ka pulled the finger-sized glowrod from a pouch at her belt and ignited it to light her way. Black crystalline sand crunched under her feet and glittered like thousands of fiery sparks, throwing back the light of her glowrod. As she trudged farther in, the sandy floor became hard rock, glassy like obsidian. Ahead of her the rocky corridor radiated an eerie red light, and the heat grew stifling.

Occasionally she heard a rumbling, rushing roar, as if the volcano itself were breathing deeply in its sleep. The stony walls around her took on a cracked, broken look. Some of the larger fissures ran from floor to ceiling and leaked puffs of acrid white steam. But she saw no embedded crystals.

The lava tube wound on and on. Losing patience, Tenel Ka had just about decided to turn back when she rounded one last corner and encountered a wave of searing heat. She had found what she was looking for.

"Ah," she said. "Aha."

She wouldn't be able to bear the heat for long, but she had to risk it. On the floor of the tunnel lay a huge slab of glossy black rock that had broken free from a crack on the tunnel wall. Ripples of scorching air danced before her in the dimness. Rivulets of perspiration ran down her forehead and into her eyes, blurring her vision. Even so, she could not mistake the chunks of spiky crystals that grew on the broken slab, glittering and hazy.

The rock surrounding her was too hot to touch, so Tenel Ka worked quickly. Holding her glowrod in her teeth, she pulled a small scrap of lizard hide from a pouch at her belt, wrapped it around a clump of the crystals, used her grappling hook to chip away at a few of the crystals, then pried them loose.

Tenel Ka tucked the crystals, still wrapped in their protective lizard hide, into her belt pouch, then headed back up the tunnel at a trot. Holding the glowrod high above her head, she raised her voice in a loud ululating cry of triumph that echoed down the length of the lava tube.

Back in her quarters, Tenel Ka sat at a low wooden table with the components of her future lightsaber spread in front of her. Everything she needed for assembling her weapon was here: switches, crystals, the covering plate, a power source, a focusing lens, and the rancor-tooth hilt.

She ran a light fingertip over the intricate battle etchings she had carved on the ivory lightsaber handle. The markings had turned out even better than she had hoped.

After returning from her crystal hunt, she had applied to the rancor tooth a paste made of dampened black sand from the floor of the lava tube. When she polished the tooth to a soft luster, pigment from the dark sand had stained every crevice of her carving to bring each etched line into sharp relief. The decorated rancor tooth was a beautiful piece, worthy of a warrior.

A yawn of contented weariness escaped her lips as Tenel Ka began to piece the components together according to Master Skywalker's directions. She frowned when she realized that the hollow inside the rancor's tooth was not quite large enough to contain the arrangement of crystals she had hoped for. She frowned again when she noticed on close inspection that each of her hazy crystals contained a tiny flaw. She suppressed another yawn and shook her head in resignation. Well, she didn't have much choice. There hadn't been time to examine the crystals more carefully in the searing lava tube, and now it was too late to search for more.

Tenel Ka thought back over the past two weeks, the drills and exercises she had put herself through. Her reflexes were lightning-fast, her skills and senses sharp as a laser. She shrugged, trying to loosen the knot of weary tension that had crept into her shoulders. She would have to make do. After all, in the long run it was the warrior and not the weapon that determined victory.

She nodded to herself as she picked up the lightsaber handle and began placing the components inside.

4

THE JUNGLE CLEARING was alive with thousands—no, millions!—of living creatures and interesting plants, strangely colorful mushrooms and droning insects, all of which offered great distractions to Jacen. He had to work very hard to keep his mind from wandering. At the moment it was far more important to pay attention to Luke Skywalker as he set up the first lightsaber dueling exercise for the young Jedi Knights.

During the construction of their weapons, the trainees had sparred with dueling droids and with each other, using sticks the same length as a lightsaber blade. After completing their lightsabers, they had spent a week practicing with their real weapons against stationary targets, accustoming themselves to the feel of the energy blades.

Now, though, Master Skywalker had deemed them ready to move on to the next step.

The clearing was a burned-out spot where lightning had sparked a brief but intense forest fire. The jungle dampness and lush foliage had quickly smothered the blaze, but a huge Massassi tree—its trunk charred and weakened by the searing flames—had toppled over, taking with it several smaller trees and bushes. The rest of the clearing was a matted maze of pale green undergrowth—weeds and grasses and flowers attempting to reclaim the burned and crumbly soil.

Because today's exercises would be both mental and physical, Uncle Luke wore a comfortable flight suit, as did Jacen and Jaina. Tenel Ka's ever-present reptilian armor left her arms and legs bare, giving her complete freedom of movement. Her long reddish-gold hair had been plaited into intricate braids, with special ornamentation on each one. Lowbacca wore no garment other than his belt, woven of strands he had harvested from a deadly syren plant in the deep forests on Kashyyyk. Em Teedee hung in his accustomed place at the Wookiee's waist.

All of the young Jedi Knights carried something new and special this time, though—their own lightsabers, completed after weeks of delicate construction.

While Jacen stood with his friends, flicking occasional glances in the direction of rustling leaves that hinted at the presence of strange creatures, Luke Skywalker took a seat on the massive fallen trunk. At last he unslung the mysterious pack he had lugged all the way from the Great Temple.

"What's in there, Uncle Luke?" Jacen asked, unable to restrain his curiosity. Since he couldn't investigate the interesting insects and plants, he needed to focus his mind on something else.

Luke gave a secretive smile and withdrew a scarlet sphere the size of a large ball, perfectly smooth except for tiny covered openings that might have been repulsorjets or small targeting lasers. Luke set the ball on the slanted, burned trunk; miraculously, it did not roll down the slope, but remained exactly where he had placed it. He withdrew another of the scarlet spheres, and another, and another.

"Remotes!" Jaina cried, guessing what they were. "Those *are* remotes, aren't they, Uncle Luke? What are they for?"

"Target practice," he said. All four remotes sat balanced on the burned Massassi trunk, refusing to roll, as if they could ignore gravity.

Lowbacca grunted with surprise, and Tenel Ka straightened. "We are going to shoot at them?"

"No," Luke said. "They're going to shoot at *you*."

"And we deflect the shots with our lightsabers?" Jacen asked.

"Yes," Luke said, "but it's not as easy as you might think."

"I never said I thought it would be *easy*," Jacen muttered.

Tenel Ka nodded. "A lesson to sharpen our

reflexes and concentration. We must react quickly to intercept each burst from the remotes."

"Ah, but it gets harder," Luke said. He reached into the sack again, removed a flexible helmet with a transparisteel visor tinted a deep red, and handed it to Tenel Ka. "You'll each wear these." He withdrew another pair of helmets for the twins, but the last one consisted of only a red visor fastened with crude tie-straps. "Sorry, Lowbacca, but I couldn't find a helmet big enough for your head. This will have to do."

Jacen slipped the helmet over his perpetually tousled brown hair and suddenly saw the jungle through a scarlet filter. The thick forest held a more primeval quality now, as if backlit with smoldering fires. The details were duller, darker, and Jacen wondered what the helmet and visor were supposed to do—protect them against stray shots from the remotes? He looked over at where the bright red remotes had rested on the burned tree trunk . . . or rather where they should have been.

Jacen blinked. "Hey, they're gone!"

"Not gone," Luke said. "Just invisible. When you look at the remotes through the red filters, you can't see them anymore." Luke smiled. "That's the point. When Obi-Wan Kenobi taught me, he made me fight using a helmet with the blast shield down. I couldn't see a thing. You'll at least be able to see your surroundings . . . but not the remotes."

Jacen wanted to ask how he was supposed to fight what he couldn't see, but he knew what Uncle Luke would say.

"I didn't want you totally blind," Luke continued, "because all four of you will be training here in the clearing with different remotes. This way you'll be able to see *each other*. I don't want anyone getting too enthusiastic and causing injuries instead of just deflecting laser bolts."

This brought a small chuckle from Jacen and Jaina, but Master Skywalker looked at all of the trainees sternly. "I wasn't kidding," he said. "A lightsaber can cut through practically any substance known—and that includes people. Remember this warning: lightsabers are not toys. They are dangerous weapons. Treat them with the utmost care and respect. I hope that the time you each spent building your lightsaber has taught you more about its power and its risks."

Luke picked up a set of controls. "Now let's see how well you work with the Force and your own energy blades."

He flipped a switch, and Jacen heard a hissing, whirring sound. But he saw nothing until he pushed up the scarlet visor. The four remotes drifted into the air, spinning around and scanning the vicinity.

"These lasers are low power," Luke said, "but don't think they won't sting if you get hit by one."

Jacen muttered to his sister, "At least he's not

throwing rocks or knives at us, like at the Shadow Academy."

"Visors down," Luke said. "Take your positions."

The companions spread out in the clearing, tramping down the weedy underbrush.

"Ignite your lightsabers," Luke said, then sat back. He seemed to be enjoying himself.

As one, the four Jedi trainees held out the handles of their new weapons and depressed the power studs. Brilliant beams sprang out in the red dimness, bright slashes the length of a sword blade burning through the thick crimson in front of Jacen's eyes. The tinted masks drained all other color from their lightsabers, transforming them into glowing red rods. It reminded Jacen of Darth Vader's weapon.

"The remotes are circling now," Luke said. "In the next thirty seconds they'll begin to fire at random. Reach out with the Force. *Feel* them. Sense the impending attack—then use your lightsaber blade to deflect it. A lot of your training has been leading up to this. Let's see how well you do."

Jacen tensed, holding his lightsaber ready. Much as he hated to admit it, he drew upon some of the skills Brakiss had taught him at the Shadow Academy. He felt the energy blade humming in his hand, pulsing with power. The sharpness of ozone reached his nostrils. He heard his friends moving about, preparing for an attack that could come from any direction.

The buzzing lightsabers muted all other sounds, just as the red filter drowned all other colors. Suddenly Jacen heard a snapping shot, though he saw nothing. A loud Wookiee yowl preceded the vibrating hum of a lightsaber blade sweeping sideways and hitting nothing. Lowie roared again.

"Dear me, Master Lowbacca, that wasn't even close," Em Teedee exclaimed. "I do hope you'll improve significantly with practice."

Lowie snarled, sounding hurt, and Em Teedee responded in a somewhat cowed fashion, "Well, all right. I understand it's more difficult since you can't *see* anything. . . . Even so, I should think it inadvisable to allow it to strike you again."

Jacen's interest in the conversation vanished when a sizzling bolt shot out from behind and struck him squarely on the backside. He yelped with pain. The tiny wound burned as badly as if a stinger lizard had zapped him. He whirled, slashing with the lightsaber, but by then it was too late.

From across the clearing another bolt shot out, followed by a crash of underbrush. Through the visor he saw Tenel Ka leap to one side. A branch snapped in two as the invisible laser struck it where Tenel Ka had stood only seconds before. The warrior girl crouched, holding her lightsaber up, her head cocked in concentration.

Jacen reached out with his mind, trying to sense through the Force where his remote would shoot next. He heard two more laser blasts and then a *spang* as Jaina successfully deflected one of the bolts. Jacen focused on the pain at the spot where he had been struck by the laser, using it to intensify his determination. He didn't want to be stung again.

Another laser beam shot out. He swiped the lightsaber at it, barely missing—though his motion was enough to shift him out of its path so that the beam sizzled past. He felt the warmth of its passage, but could not see it.

"That was close," he said, then instinctively swung to strike again as the remote fired once more.

Jaina parried a flurry of bolts as her remote attacked mercilessly, firing five times in rapid succession. One of her bolts ricocheted off the glowing edge of her lightsaber directly toward Jacen. He responded without conscious thought, using the Force and flowing with it, somehow knowing what to do as he shifted his own blade sideways just enough to catch the diverted bolt. The deflected blast bounced up into the trees, where it fried a fistful of leaves.

In a single follow-through motion, Jacen spun, reaching up with the lightsaber blade to ward off a second bolt fired from the other remote hovering in front of them.

Lowbacca bellowed with triumph as he, too, got the hang of defending himself.

Except for her heavy breathing, Tenel Ka was

quiet, thoughtful. Through the red filter Jacen watched as she parried one of the lasers and leaped upward with all her might, using her lightsaber like a cleaver. A shower of sparks erupted and a smoking hole appeared in midair. Jacen heard a *thunk* as pieces of Tenel Ka's remote fell useless to the jungle floor.

"All right. That's enough for now," Luke Skywalker said.

Tenel Ka switched off her weapon and stood with her hands on her hips, her elbows spread. Jacen flipped up his red visor to discover his own remote hovering barely at arm's length in front of his face. He stepped back, startled.

Tenel Ka's remote lay on the ground sliced in two, its circuits flickering and sparking. Jaina and Lowie also shut off their weapons and stood panting and grinning. Jacen rubbed the burning pain in his backside and grimaced sheepishly, hoping none of the others would notice.

"Excellent, all of you—except now it looks as if I'll need a new remote," Luke said, smiling wryly at Tenel Ka. "You did very well with the Force."

"Not only with the Force," she said, thrusting her chin upward and squaring her shoulders. "I also used my ears to track the remote. When I concentrated, I could hear it even above the sound of the lightsabers."

Luke chuckled. "Good. A Jedi *should* use all available skills and resources."

* * *

Jaina gripped the lightsaber in both hands and positioned the brilliant, electric-violet blade in front of her. She looked past the searing line of controlled fire at Lowbacca, her opponent, who stood opposite her, a lightsaber in his hairy grasp. He growled his readiness.

Jaina looked into the young Wookiee's golden eyes, saw the dark streak of black fur swirling up from his eyebrow and around his head. She swallowed and tensed. Though lanky, Lowbacca was much taller than she, and Jaina knew he was about three times as strong. But in his furry expression she saw an uncertainty, a genuine discomfort that mirrored her own.

"Do I really *have* to fight Lowie, Uncle—uh, Master Skywalker?" Jaina asked.

Luke Skywalker stood. "You're not fighting him, Jaina. You're *fencing* with him. Test your opponent. Gauge each other's skills. Learn to judge reactions. Explore strategies. But be careful."

Jaina thought of her training at the Shadow Academy and how she and Jacen had dueled with lightsabers, not realizing that they had fought each other in holographic disguise.

"Remember," Luke cautioned, "a Jedi fights only as a last resort. If you are forced to draw your lightsaber, you have already forfeited much of your advantage. A Jedi trusts the Force and at first seeks other ways to resolve problems: patience, logic, tolerance, attentive listening, negotiation, persuasion, calming techniques.

"But there are times when a Jedi *must* fight. Knowing that the Shadow Academy is out there, I fear those times will come all too often for us. And so you must learn how to wield your lightsabers."

He stepped back and motioned to Jacen and Tenel Ka, who waited on the edge of the clearing, sitting next to each other on the burned tree trunk. "You two will be next. Jaina, don't worry about Lowie being so much bigger and stronger than you are. Dueling with a lightsaber is primarily skill, and I think you're equally matched in that. Your one true disadvantage is that his reach is much longer than yours. Unfortunately," Luke said with a sigh, "circumstances don't always pit us against equal opponents. As for you, Lowie, be careful not to underestimate Jaina."

He dropped back to watch. "Now, show me what you can do."

"Well?" Jaina stepped forward, keeping her gaze locked with Lowie's. "What are we waiting for?"

The Wookiee shifted his lightsaber, bringing its molten-bronze blade into position. Jaina moved hers up to meet it, crossing her blade against his. She felt the pressure, the sizzling of sparks, and the discharge as the powerful beams drove against each other. She saw the muscles bulging in Lowie's long arms as he strained against her—but Jaina held her own.

"All right, let's try something else." Jaina withdrew her lightsaber, then swung it at her Wookiee friend slowly, cautiously—and Lowbacca met it with another crackle of released energy.

Swinging to strike again, she said, "This isn't so bad."

Lowie defended himself. He seemed reluctant to do battle.

Knowing that Lowie had endured horrifying struggles at the Shadow Academy—and remembering again that she had been forced to fight her own brother—Jaina realized that Brakiss and the violet-eyed Tamith Kai would stop at nothing to bring down the New Republic. She and Lowie would both be needed to defend against the Dark Jedi. She decided now that the best way to rid Lowie of his reservations would be to go on the offensive.

And this time she did not feel strangled by darkness. Today Jaina fought with full willingness, learning to be a defender of the light side, a champion of the Force. Uncle Luke had been correct in his speech in front of the Jedi trainees. She knew in her heart that the Shadow Academy had only begun to cause trouble, and she would have to fight to get her friend Zekk freed.

But first she had to learn how.

Lowbacca responded with greater strength, a better show of his abilities, as he parried her blows and struck back with his own. She had to move quickly to cross blades with him again. They clashed and struck. Sparks flew.

Lowie spun and chopped down, but she met his lightsaber with hers, smiling, intently focused. She heard Jacen cheering from the side.

"Excellent, Master Lowbacca!" Em Teedee said. "Now do be careful—you wouldn't want a flying spark to damage me."

Jaina felt the Force flowing through her; Lowbacca wore an expression of exhilaration on his furry face. He opened his mouth, showing fangs and letting out a bellow of challenge—not mean or angry, simply an outpouring of excitement.

Lowie grasped the handle of his large lightsaber with both hands and swept sideways, attempting to catch Jaina by surprise—but she turned the tables on him. Summoning a burst of energy, she astonished the Wookiee by leaping high into the air up to the level of Lowie's head. His lightsaber swept harmlessly beneath her, and she landed lightly on the weed-covered ground behind him, laughing and panting.

"Oh my! That was *most* unexpected," Em Teedee said. "Splendid work, Mistress Jaina."

"Hey, that was great, Jaina!" her twin brother called.

Lowie raised his lightsaber in salute. Jaina grinned, her eyes gleaming.

"Most impressive," Luke said, turning to Jacen and Tenel Ka. "Next, let's see how well our spectators can do."

5

TENEL KA HESITATED, rubbing her fingers along the ivory surface of the rancor-tooth lightsaber handle. She held the deactivated weapon in front of her, drawing deep breaths. Intent on her body, her surroundings, she tightened her muscles and brought them to full readiness. Jungle sounds filled the clearing: the whisper of breezes ruffling leaves, the song of insects, the flutter of birds in the canopy.

She centered her thoughts, making sure her reflexes were primed and ready for action. Tenel Ka relied on her body and pressed it to its limits, but she always knew how far she could take it. So far, her muscles had never let her down.

Slowly, she opened her cool, granite-gray eyes and looked at the young man who stood in front of her, ready for the next duel.

He grinned at her. "Good against remotes is one thing, Tenel Ka," Jacen said, "but good against a real opponent? That's something else."

"This is a fact."

Depressing a button, Jacen switched on his lightsaber. The emerald-green blade sprang forth, snapping and glittering with power. "Hey, I'll try not to be too hard on you."

Tenel Ka's fingers found the recessed power button on the rancor-tooth handle. A shimmering gray-white blade extended like crackling electric fog shot through with golden sparks. The lightsaber's color reminded her of the hazy crystals she had taken from the lava tube.

"And I will try not to be too hard on you, my friend Jacen," she said. Tenel Ka tested the weapon by turning her wrist, flicking the blade from side to side. The beam sparked and sizzled as it encountered moisture in the air.

"Be careful," Master Skywalker said from his vantage point on the burned tree trunk. "Don't get cocky. You both have a great deal to learn."

"Don't worry, Uncle Luke," Jacen said. "I know it was a bad time for me, but I *did* have some training at the Shadow Academy." He grinned. "Fighting Tenel Ka will be more of a challenge than battling holographic monsters, though."

Jaina cleared her throat and spoke from where she sat, sweating and worn out after her session with Lowbacca. "And better than fighting your own sister in disguise?"

"That too," Jacen said.

Tenel Ka flicked her lightsaber back and forth again, taking a step closer to Jacen. She squared her shoulders, knowing that she stood taller than her good-humored friend. The lightsaber thrummed with power in her hand. "Are we going to talk all day, Jacen?" she said. "Or will you leave time for me to defeat you before the morning is over?"

Jacen laughed. "Hey, we're not supposed to be enemies, Tenel Ka. It's just a practice session."

She nodded. "This is a fact. Even so, we *are* opponents."

She swung her lightsaber slowly enough that he wouldn't perceive it as a real attack, but instinctively Jacen brought up his own weapon. Their blades intersected with sizzling force.

Jacen blinked in surprise, then drew back and struck against her nebulous gold-shot blade, testing. "All right then—let's go, Tenel Ka!"

She deftly sidestepped the thrust and returned with a parry of her own as he stumbled to regain his balance. Had he been a real enemy, she could have finished him then, but she pulled her blade aside for a split second, just to demonstrate that Jacen had let his guard drop—a lesson a Jedi Knight would need to learn to avoid defeat.

Unexpectedly, Jacen whirled and came up with a backhanded strike that forced her to retaliate. "I figure we should do something about that lack of confidence you've got, Tenel Ka," Jacen said, still grinning.

"I have no such lack," she said, and found that

perspiration had broken out on her forehead. She swung, and Jacen caught her blow on his blade, laughing. She noted the degree of strength he used, the speed with which he maneuvered his weapon. They clashed again. Her cheerful friend, usually so scattered and disorganized, was giving her a surprisingly difficult workout.

"Hey, Tenel Ka," Jacen said as he struck twice more, as if he always held conversations while fighting with a lightsaber, "you know why a wampa snow monster has such long arms?" He paused for just a beat. "Because his hands are so far away from his body!"

Lowbacca groaned with miserable laughter, prompting the little droid at his waist to speak up in a tinny voice. "I fail to perceive the amusement value in Jacen's explanation of a zoological anomaly," Em Teedee said.

"Your jokes cannot distract me, Jacen," Tenel Ka said, swinging her lightsaber once more. Did he really think he could break her concentration so easily? "I do not find them humorous."

Jacen sighed as he met her blade with his own. "I know. I've been trying to get you to laugh ever since I've known you."

Tenel Ka watched her opponent closely, trying to judge from the tension in his muscles how soon he intended to make a surprise move, in which direction he would react, when the motion of his blade was a genuine attack and when it was merely a feint.

"Good," Master Skywalker said from where he watched. "Feel the Force. The lightsaber is not just a weapon. It is an extension of yourself."

Jacen pressed Tenel Ka hard, and she skipped backward a couple of paces. It was obvious he was trying to drive her toward an outcropping of broken boulders at the edge of the clearing. Jacen must have thought she had forgotten about them, but Tenel Ka filed away every detail of her surroundings in her mind.

Just as she reached the rocks, Jacen gave away his plans even more clearly with a broad grin. He pushed forward abruptly, no doubt expecting her to trip. But Tenel Ka leaped lightly backward over the boulders and landed on the other side, her legs planted firmly in a fighting stance. Suddenly foiled, Jacen stumbled and fell toward her, almost hitting the rocks himself. He came up sputtering in disbelief.

"Hey," he said, then smiled. "Good one!"

Tenel Ka stood waiting for him, her braided hair dangling about her head, drenched with sweat. Allowing herself a brief moment of self-indulgence, she switched the lightsaber to her left hand to prove she could fight just as well with either arm. She had practiced equally with her left and right hands, knowing it might prove a useful skill sometime.

"Show-off," Jacen said. After a heartbeat of hesitation, he switched his own blade to his left hand and charged at her, swinging hard with the emerald-green lightsaber. She raised her own misty-white and gold blade, struck at him, then struck again. Sparks flew as the blades met.

When Jacen laughed with exhilaration, she allowed herself a satisfied grin as well. "You are a good opponent, Jacen Solo," she said.

"You bet I am," he answered.

Tenel Ka knew that her skill was based on her prowess, her physical ability. Though she had constructed a fine lightsaber, she would become a great warrior because of her *fighting abilities*, not because of the strength of any weapon, no matter how powerful.

Jacen's lightsaber pressed against hers, and she took a step back. They stood deadlocked, slamming energy blade against impenetrable energy blade. Fiery electricity crackled, and the air thickened with the sharp scent of ozone. Tenel Ka pushed with all her strength, but Jacen countered with equal force.

Her palm was sweaty, but her hand maintained its grip on the rancor-tooth handle. Inside, the components of her lightsaber vibrated, as if struggling to maintain the full energy of the blade while Tenel Ka pressed so furiously against an equally powerful weapon. She pushed harder. The handle rattled.

Jacen grinned at her. "Hope you don't expect me to surrender too easily."

"Perhaps you should," she panted, and pressed harder, ignoring the strange, unsettling sensations from her weapon. She gritted her teeth. Her arm strained. The lightsabers whined and buzzed. Jacen shoved back with all his might. His eyes glittered with the effort.

Over by the edge of the clearing, Master Skywalker stood watching the tense battle, as did Lowbacca and Jaina.

Tenel Ka narrowed her gray eyes, not easing up for an instant, wondering how best she could defeat Jacen and end this match.

Suddenly, something changed inside her lightsaber. She heard a sharp crack and then a loud hissing sizzle.

Jacen pressed harder with his emerald-green blade. For the briefest instant, the golden sparks that shot through her white pulsating energy beam flickered wildly. Her blade blurred with static, grew less focused.

Intent on the battle, Jacen gave a final, extra push with all his strength.

It happened all at once.

The power source in Tenel Ka's lightsaber gave a shriek of electrical overload—and the blade winked out like a snuffed candle. Sparks and smoke poured from the end of the handle where an energy blade should have glowed.

Suddenly, encountering no resistance as Jacen

thrust with his last reserves of strength, the emerald-green lightsaber sliced through the opening where Tenel Ka's own blade had been just a moment before—plunging down to the only thing that stood in its way.

Tenel Ka felt a line of blazing agony sweep across her arm just above the elbow. It *burned* . . . and yet below the burn she felt only a sickening, horrible coldness—a bone-deep chill like none she had ever felt before.

Somehow her lightsaber thumped on the ground with a soft *thud*. Impossibly, she saw her hand clenching the carved rancor's tooth. Sparks the size of lightning bolts flashed around the handle as her weapon exploded in a burst of blinding light.

Bright. So very bright . . .

Tenel Ka felt a dizzying haze swirling up to engulf her. Everything was so confusing. Jacen screamed something she couldn't understand. Tenel Ka hoped intensely that she had not hurt him.

Jaina, Lowbacca, and Master Skywalker all ran toward her, shouting, but Tenel Ka couldn't find the energy to stay upright any longer. Just as Jacen reached a hand out toward her, she felt herself falling to the ground.

Then the pain and shock were completely swallowed up in blackness.

6

ON THE FRINGES of the unmapped heart of the galaxy, the Shadow Academy found a new hiding place near the flaming shells of two stars that had been dying for the last five thousand years.

Without its cloaking device, the dark Imperial training center hung like a circlet of thorns, washed in the blaze of solar radiation. The whispering trails of thrown-off star gas would camouflage the station from prying Rebel eyes.

Zekk stood before the broad windowports of the tallest observation tower, staring into the dazzling maelstrom of starfire. The darkened transparisteel of the viewport filtered out the deadly radiation— but even dimmed to a fraction of its true power, the fury of the universe left Zekk breathless.

Beside him stood Brakiss, Master of the Shadow Academy, a tall and statue-handsome Jedi. As an Imperial spy, Brakiss had once studied at the New Republic's Jedi academy; when Master Skywalker had tried to turn him away from the dark side of the Force, however, Brakiss had fled back to the Empire. There he gathered a group of Dark Jedi trainees and conditioned them to serve the great leader of the Second Imperium, the resurrected Emperor Palpatine himself.

Brakiss lifted his serene face, drinking in the view of the double suns. "This reality makes the image in my office seem like a pale glimmer by comparison, doesn't it, Zekk?"

Zekk nodded, but found himself without words.

"More than five millennia ago the Denarii Nova exploded, ripping through these stars and reducing them to cinders," Brakiss said. "The powerful Sith sorcerer Naga Sadow caused this cataclysmic event to gain his freedom from pursuing Republic warships. With the extravagant power of the dark side, Naga Sadow tore these two stars apart and used giant flares like two slapping hands to crush the fleet behind him."

Zekk nodded again and finally found words. "Another example of the power of the dark side."

Brakiss smiled proudly at him. "It is a power your friends Jacen and Jaina would never have shown you—much less taught you."

"No," Zekk agreed. "They never would have." For years, he had been friends with the twin children of Han Solo and Leia Organa Solo. Zekk was just a street kid, though—a nobody, who lived by his wits scavenging items in the dangerous underlevels of the city-covered world of Coruscant.

His hopes for a better life had been little more than dreams until the Nightsister Tamith Kai snatched him and brought him to the Shadow Academy as part of a new recruitment drive.

In an earlier attempt to gain talented candidates, Brakiss had made an error by kidnapping the high-profile trainees Jacen, Jaina, and Lowbacca. When that failed, he had decided the Shadow Academy might do better with a different sort of person: downtrodden young ones who wouldn't be missed, yet had just as much potential to acquire Jedi powers—and more to gain by swearing allegiance to the Second Imperium.

Zekk had resisted the transformation at first, fighting to stay loyal to his friends. But gradually Brakiss lured him, showing Zekk how to use the Force for one small thing, then another. Zekk discovered that he was strong in the Force, and he learned quickly.

The experience altered his feelings toward the twins from friendship to resentment. Jaina and Jacen had never thought to include him in Jedi testing, though he felt he had as much innate talent as any of their highborn friends. Zekk's main regret in leaving his old life was that he missed his companion, old Peckhum. But now he had much more of a future. Zekk was beginning to understand Jedi powers, and he had already done things he'd never dreamed of.

Gazing at the stormy suns, Brakiss raised his arms to each side, spreading his fingers. His silvery robe flowed around him as if knit from silken spiderwebs. He stared into the swirling flares of the Denarii Nova. "Observe, Zekk—and learn."

Closing his eyes, the Master of the Shadow Academy began to move his hands. Zekk watched through the observation port, his green eyes widening.

The ocean of rarefied incandescent gases between the dying stars started to swirl like arms of fire . . . writhing, changing shape, dancing in time with the hand motions Brakiss made. The dark teacher was manipulating the starfire itself!

He whispered to Zekk without opening his eyes, without observing the effect of his work. "The Force is in all things," Brakiss said, "from the smallest pebble to the largest star. This is just a glimmer of how Naga Sadow reached out to the stars and delivered a mortal wound five thousand years ago."

"Could you make the sun explode?" Zekk asked in awe.

Brakiss opened his eyes and looked at his young student. His smooth, perfect forehead creased. "I don't know," he said. "And I don't believe I ever want to try."

Zekk remembered the way Brakiss had first enticed him to experiment with his innate Jedi powers, by giving him a flarestick and showing how simple it was to draw shapes in the flames with the Force. Here in the Denarii Nova, Brakiss had done the same thing—only on a scale the size of a star system.

"Could I try it?" Zekk said eagerly, leaning forward. He touched his fingertips to the light-filtering viewport, looking out at the double star and its brilliant corona, which rippled like a barely contained inferno.

Brakiss smiled again. "You're ambitious as always, young Zekk." He placed a firm hand on his prize student's shoulder. "But do not be impatient. There is more you must learn, much more. You've been such a voracious learner, surpassing my greatest expectations about how capable you are of using the power you were born with. You easily accomplish the exercises I set for you—but there comes a time when every Jedi trainee must be tested to the limit." Brakiss raised his eyebrows. "Tamith Kai continues to flaunt her greatest student, Vilas, who has been training here for more than a year. But you are learning so much faster. I believe you have reached that stage, Zekk."

He reached into his silvery robes and grasped something there, but hesitated, meeting the dark-haired boy's steady gaze. "I know you are ready for this. Do not disappoint me."

"What is it, Master Brakiss?" Zekk asked.

From the folds of his robe Brakiss removed a dark, ornate cylinder. "The time has come for you to have your own lightsaber."

Zekk took the ancient Jedi weapon and stared at it in wonder. Even deactivated, it felt powerful in his hand. He squeezed the grip and swung the handle back and forth, imagining a crackling energy blade. It felt good. Very good.

"Normally," Brakiss said, "I would have suggested that you build your own weapon. But it takes time and intense concentration to assemble the components, understand the workings. And we have not the time. Through the dark side, many things are easier, more efficient. Take this lightsaber as my gift to you; wield it well in the service of the Second Imperium."

"May I turn on the power?" Zekk whispered, still in awe.

"Of course."

Brakiss stood back as Zekk activated the lightsaber. A scarlet beam lanced outward, glowing like lava. "This is a masterful weapon," Brakiss said. "It has already been attuned for use by the dark side."

Zekk swiveled his wrist left and right, listening to the hum of the powerful cutting edge.

"In fact, this lightsaber is very similar to the one Darth Vader used," Brakiss pointed out.

Zekk struck out against the air. "When can I train with it?" he said. "How will I learn?"

Brakiss led the young man out of the observation tower. "We have simulation rooms," he said. "A while ago, I spent some time training your friends Jacen and Jaina. Very disappointing. They did learn how to use lightsabers, but they resisted me each step of the way.

"I expect you, on the other hand, to excel in every routine. *You,* Zekk, will quickly surpass anything your friends accomplished. And I know Master Skywalker and his fears—he is too nervous to train his precious younger students with their own lightsabers. He considers the energy blades too dangerous." Brakiss laughed. "His fears are misplaced. The most truly dangerous thing is a Dark Jedi *wielding* such a weapon."

As Zekk accompanied his teacher down the corridor, he switched off the lightsaber and held its sturdy handle in his grip. He looked down at the legendary Jedi weapon and ran his finger over its case.

The lightsaber felt warm, ready . . . begging to be used. The afterimage of the scarlet blade still blazed across his vision.

Zekk tried to blink it away, but the bright line remained. At last he said, "Yes, I can see how such a weapon could be very dangerous indeed."

7

JACEN COULDN'T HELP brooding as he wandered aimlessly through the halls of the Jedi academy, keeping to the shadowy corridors that were least used by other students. Jaina walked beside him in stunned silence, as she had for the past two hours. She seemed to need her brother's company as much as he needed hers, though neither of them knew quite what to say.

Jacen still couldn't understand why Uncle Luke hadn't allowed anyone else to stay with the unconscious Tenel Ka while the medical droid tended her. Neither had he allowed anyone to be present when he went to the Comm Center to contact Tenel Ka's family and inform them of the accident.

Uncle Luke himself had scooped up Tenel Ka's limp form and rushed her back to the Great Temple. As the twins hurried behind, Jacen had sensed the Jedi Master drawing on the Force to help the injured young woman maintain her strength, as well as to move faster and to keep from jarring her. At the same time, he had sent a continuous stream of soothing thoughts toward Tenel Ka's unconscious mind, thoughts of peace and healing.

Jacen had known he should try to do the same, to help his friend in any way he could, but his thoughts were in such a turmoil that he was afraid his attempts would only make things worse. Perhaps that was why Master Skywalker hadn't let any of them stay with the warrior girl once they returned to the Great Temple. He had assured the friends that he would call instantly if Tenel Ka asked for them.

Since then, the twins had roamed up and down stairways and dim passages, both of them alone with their private thoughts. When Lowie joined them without a word, neither asked where he had been. After all, he often went out to the tall trees alone, to sit and think about his home on Kashyyyk, his parents, his younger sister. . . . Now he was ready to be with friends again. But Jacen was not surprised to note, when he glanced down at Em Teedee, that the little droid had been shut off.

They were all disturbed by what had happened—no one more so than Jacen. He replayed the scene over and over in his mind as they walked: the sizzling, popping sound of the lightsabers as they clashed, the look of challenge in Tenel Ka's eyes, the glowing green of his own energy blade passing *through* hers. . . . He squeezed his eyes shut in an effort to block the rest from his mind, but that was a mistake. The scene was too vivid in his memory. His eyes flew open again.

"I can't wait any longer," he choked. "I have to see Tenel Ka to make sure she's all right—and to apologize to her."

"We'll go with you," Jaina said. Lowie purred his agreement.

When the three Jedi trainees reached the room where their friend had been treated, they saw Luke Skywalker emerging, Artoo-Detoo at his side.

"How's Tenel Ka?" Jacen asked immediately. "Is she awake? Can we see her?"

Luke Skywalker hesitated, and Jacen could see the concern written on his face. "She's still recovering from the . . . shock," he said. "She *is* awake now, but she's not quite ready to see you yet."

"But a time like this is when she needs her friends most," Jaina said.

Artoo-Detoo swiveled the top of his domed head back and forth once and buzzed an emphatic negative.

"But I have to see her," Jacen objected. "I need to do *something* for her—tell her jokes, hold her hand. . . . Blaster bolts! She only *has* one hand now, and I'm the one who's responsible."

Artoo gave a low mournful whistle, and Luke looked at his nephew in sympathy. "I know this is hard for you," he said, "but it's even harder for Tenel Ka. I remember the thoughts that went through my head when I lost my own hand on Cloud City, fighting with Darth Vader. I had just learned that he was my father. It felt as if I had lost a part of myself, a part of who I was . . . and then I lost my hand, too."

"But hands can be fixed," Jaina pointed out. "They can be reattached and healed in bacta tanks."

Luke shook his head. "My hand was gone. There was nothing to reattach."

"But your synthetic hand works just as well as your old one did," Jacen said.

"Perhaps," Luke said, flexing his lifelike prosthetic and running the artificial thumb along his fingertips, "but it was a difficult decision to make. I remember thinking that maybe I had just taken another step toward becoming more like my father, like Darth Vader—partly alive, but partly a machine. Tenel Ka will have to face the same decision herself. When her lightsaber exploded, it destroyed any chance we had of reattaching that arm."

"Uncle Luke, I need to see her," Jacen pleaded. "I *have* to apologize."

Luke squeezed his shoulder. "I promise to call you the moment she's ready to talk. Try to get some rest now."

Jacen slept fitfully, tossing and turning as images of a wounded Tenel Ka haunted his dreams.

"We are opponents," he heard her say.

"No. I'm your friend," Jacen tried to answer, but *his voice was trapped in his throat; he could make*

no sound. He felt again the sickening jolt as her lightsaber dissolved beneath his and the sizzling green energy blade sliced through her arm.

The smell of singed flesh clawed at his nostrils. The sound of her exploding rancor-tooth weapon crashed against his eardrums, and his vision filled with the image of Tenel Ka's cool gray eyes, clouded with accusation.

"We are opponents. . . ."

Jacen felt something push at his mind, and he woke drenched in sweat, his single light blanket damp and tangled around his legs. He wasn't quite certain what had awakened him, but he knew it was somehow urgent. *It's Tenel Ka. She needs us.* The thought came unbidden to his mind. Through his open window, from the direction of the jungle he heard the faint ululating howl of a Wookiee.

Jumping from his sleeping pallet, he hurriedly fastened the front of the rumpled orange flight suit he had never quite bothered to take off when he'd lain on his bed. The distant howl came again, and Jacen could sense that Lowie, meditating at the top of a high Massassi tree, must be trying to tell him something. Without bothering to put on a pair of boots, he bolted out of his room and called at his sister's doorway.

"Jaina, wake up. Something's wrong." He raced on down the hallway, not waiting for her reply. But something—perhaps Lowie's call—had already wakened his sister, because he hadn't even turned the corner before he heard Jaina running down the hall after him. He didn't slow, though. Bare feet slapping against the cold flagstones, he rushed out the nearest exit and down one of the Great Temple's external stairways, taking the torch-lit steps three at a time. He felt the nudge against his mind again and headed in the direction it had come from: the landing pad.

As he rounded the corner of the temple, with Jaina hard on his heels, he was surprised to see Lowie coming toward them from the jungle, where eerie night mists blanketed the ground with translucent white. On the landing field, though, Jacen saw something that surprised him even more.

A small, sleek shuttle, about half the size of the *Millennium Falcon*, lifted off the grassy stubble of the landing pad, blasting away wisps of ground fog. And there, bathed in the blue glow from the landing lights, his hair whipping wildly in the breeze, stood Luke Skywalker.

The Jedi Master was facing the shuttle, one arm raised as if in farewell, as the three young Jedi Knights raced up to him. Jacen and Jaina spoke at the same moment.

"Who was that?"

"What's going on?"

The tall, gangly Wookiee added a questioning bark of his own.

Luke Skywalker lowered his eyes to look at his Jedi students.

"It was Tenel Ka, wasn't it?" Jacen persisted, without really needing to hear the answer. In the dimness, his gaze locked with his uncle's, and the Jedi Master nodded.

"Her family insisted on coming immediately to pick her up. She should be in good hands now—don't worry."

Jacen felt as if a bantha had just stepped on his chest. He struggled for enough breath to speak. He felt betrayed. "She's gone! You said you'd call us when Tenel Ka was ready to see us."

Luke Skywalker cleared his throat. "She wasn't ready."

Lowie gave a despairing groan.

"But we didn't even get a chance to say good-bye," Jaina said.

Her uncle sighed. "I know. But she's with family now. They'll take care of her."

Jacen saw his sister shake her head in confusion. "But how can that be true?" Her question made no sense to him, and he looked at her, waiting for her to explain. "What I mean is," she went on, "why would Tenel Ka's family from Dathomir come for her in *that* shuttle?"

Jacen shrugged, feeling as if she expected him to understand. He didn't. "What's so strange about it?" he asked finally.

"That was an *Express*-class ambassadorial shuttle," she said. "And it had the markings of the Royal House of Hapes."

Three pairs of questioning eyes turned toward Luke Skywalker.

8

THE PASSENGERS' QUARTERS aboard the Hapan royal shuttle *Thunder Wraith* were spacious and equipped with every convenience a space traveler could desire. The elegant appointments of the cabin fell just short of ostentation; the chief adornment on each wall consisted of an ornate gilt frame surrounding a massive viewscreen.

Tenel Ka took no notice of the spectacular view, however. She had seen hyperspace before. She had no desire to see anything. Or anyone.

Or to *feel* anything. Numb. That was what she felt. Mind, emotions . . . even her arm. All numb.

The thought crossed her mind briefly that perhaps she ought to eat something. She'd had no food since before . . . since *before*.

No, she decided. No food. She could not work up enthusiasm for eating, or anything else, for that matter.

Her reddish-gold braids hung in tangled disarray around her face. Though the medical droid had done a serviceable job of washing her body and disinfecting the wound before cauterizing it, the droid had no programming on what to do with hair. It had kindly offered to shave Tenel Ka's head for her, but she had declined. One of the twins might have been willing to help her comb through the mess and rebraid it. But she'd been too proud to let her friends see her in her current condition, afraid of the disgust she might see on their faces—or worse yet, pity.

At least that was one good thing about having been spirited away from Yavin 4 in the middle of the night, Tenel Ka thought: she didn't have to see anyone, and so would be spared both sympathy and derision.

As if to dispel Tenel Ka's only comforting thought, Ambassador Yfra chose that moment to appear. Her grandmother's aging henchwoman, for all her kindly smiles and refined features, was still cut from the same cloth as the former queen—power-hungry and more than willing to do whatever it took to add to her personal power. Not long ago, Yfra had tried to visit Yavin 4, but when her friends were kidnapped by the Shadow Academy, Tenel Ka had gone with Master Skywalker to rescue them. Tenel Ka had not been disappointed to miss the ambassador, who had canceled the visit. She had never trusted the woman and disliked her instinctively.

"Are you feeling any better, my dear?" the

ambassador said with nauseating insincerity. "Would you like to talk?"

"No," Tenel Ka said stubbornly. "Thank you." Then curiosity began to tickle her numbed brain, and she asked, "Why were you the one chosen to bring me home?"

"Actually," Yfra said, not meeting Tenel Ka's eyes, "I wasn't so much *chosen* as I was . . . convenient. I was in a nearby star system on business, you see, when your grandmother received word of your . . . unfortunate accident.

"Now, my dear," she continued, "we'll be coming out of hyperspace in a few hours, so if there's anything I can do in the meantime—"

"Yes, there is," Tenel Ka interrupted in her usual forthright manner. "I wish to be left alone."

If the ambassador was put off by the abrupt answer, she covered it well. "Why, of course you do, my dear," she said with gracious insincerity. "You've been through *such* an ordeal." She looked meaningfully at Tenel Ka's arm and artfully pretended to suppress a shudder of revulsion. "You must feel simply terrible."

With that, Yfra withdrew, managing to leave Tenel Ka feeling even worse than she had before— which might actually have been what the ambassador wanted. The ruthless henchwoman was a skilled manipulator.

Tenel Ka looked at her left arm—what remained

of it, after her faulty lightsaber had exploded. There had been no chance of salvaging the limb and allowing it to heal in a bacta tank. She was no longer complete.

How could she be a true warrior now? She could not even claim her wound as the honorable result of battle. Her injury had, in fact, been caused by her own pride. And haste. And stupidity. If only she had taken more care in choosing her lightsaber components. If only she had been more meticulous in assembling the weapon. . . .

Certain that her success or failure in battle would depend on her physical skills, she had not bothered to use her best talents when constructing her weapon. Even during her Jedi training, Tenel Ka had always proudly tried to rely solely on her natural abilities, refusing to use the Force unless there was no other way to accomplish her goals.

But now what had become of her fighting prowess? How could she ever again climb a building using nothing but her fibercord, her grappling hook, and her own wits? How would she climb a tree? Or hunt? Or swim? Why, she couldn't even braid her own hair! And who would respect a Jedi with only one arm?

Lost in such grim thoughts, Tenel Ka drifted into sleep. The next thing she heard was a tapping on the door to her stateroom.

"My dear, are you resting?" Ambassador Yfra

called in her cultured voice. "Time to come out now. We're almost home. We're near Hapes."

Tenel Ka shook herself awake, stood, and looked at the viewscreens around her. The *Thunder Wraith* was no longer traveling in hyperspace. The stars and planets of the Hapes Cluster lay all about her, like handfuls of rainbow gems from Gallinore scattered on rich black velvet.

"Did you hear me, my dear?" the ambassador's voice came through the door again. "You're home."

"Home," Tenel Ka repeated. The dread she had been feeling congealed into a ball of ice in the pit of her stomach, as she considered that this place might indeed be her home from now on.

Immense warships, Hapan Battle Dragons, appeared as if out of nowhere to escort the tiny shuttle to its landing area. When the *Thunder Wraith* finally landed and Tenel Ka disembarked, she looked around with the first trace of eagerness she had felt since the lightsaber accident, searching for her parents. She was surprised, however, to find that her grandmother, Ta'a Chume, was the only relative present.

The former queen, accompanied by a large honor guard in full ceremonial garb, stepped forward to greet her granddaughter. Tenel Ka endured an embrace and a showy display of affection—although her grandmother *never* hugged her in private—and asked, "Why did my parents not come?"

"They were called away," Ta'a Chume answered smoothly, "on an urgent and top-secret diplomatic . . . matter. Only I and my most trusted confidant know their whereabouts." She motioned to one of her retainers, who strode forward to drape a royal robe across Tenel Ka's shoulders. Its thick, soft folds hid Tenel Ka's arms, and she did not have the energy to object. "But," her grandmother continued, "I assure you that your parents will return as quickly as they are able."

Four pairs of scantily clad male servants appeared, bringing cushioned seats for the princess and her grandmother. Tenel Ka sat, and only then noticed that at least two dozen more handsome servants had filed onto the landing pad. She closed her eyes and sighed. She might have known. It seemed that in her parents' absence, Ta'a Chume had decided to receive Tenel Ka with as much spectacle and fanfare as possible—perhaps to prove to her aspiring-Jedi granddaughter how wonderful it was to be a member of the royal family.

Tenel Ka was not thrilled.

Three brawny young men, dressed only in loincloths, moved to the center of the landing pad and began a rhythmic display of their gymnastic abilities. Other servants along the sidelines produced stringed instruments and flutes and began a musical accompaniment. During their performance, the former queen leaned toward her granddaughter and murmured, "You are so fortunate."

Tenel Ka blinked in surprise.

Her grandmother made an all-encompassing gesture. "Everything you see—Hapes and its sixty-three worlds—is yours to command." Her voice took on a persuasive tone. "Not many who fail to become Jedi Knights have such a pleasant alternative. After all, unlike the weapons of battle, wielding political power does not require the use of both arms."

Tenel Ka grimaced, not only at her grandmother's unfair assertion that she had failed in her Jedi training, but also because one of the acrobats had performed a double handspring—an act she had done countless times herself, and one she'd always assumed she'd go right on doing. She had even included flips, cartwheels, and handsprings in her daily exercises at the Jedi academy. The Jedi academy . . . she missed it already.

When the gymnasts finished, a young man stepped forward and began to juggle with phenomenal agility. Tenel Ka grew more uncomfortable as she watched him pass fire crystals, hoops, and blazing torches from hand to hand, tossing them high into the air with ever-increasing speed.

Another thing I will never be able to do, Tenel Ka thought, pressing her lips into a grim line.

She tried to concentrate on the juggler's face instead. The young man was indeed beautiful, but right then Tenel Ka would have traded every servant and guard on the landing platform for just a glimpse of a face that was friendly: Jacen, Jaina, Lowbacca, even Master Skywalker. . . .

"You know," her grandmother said, leaning toward her again, as if a thought had just occurred to her, "perhaps your injury was the Force's way of showing you that you were never meant to be a Jedi Knight—that your destiny has always been to rule Hapes."

Tenel Ka's breath left her in a rush, as if a rancor had stepped on her stomach. She wondered if perhaps, for once, her grandmother might not be right.

9

THE ACOUSTICS IN the grand audience chamber on Yavin 4 could carry even a whispered word from the stage to every seat in the hall. But today no lecturer stood at the far end of the long chamber, and Jaina's steps were so slow and hesitant that her booted feet made no sound. With the exception of Jacen and Lowie, who sat on stone benches near the front, the audience chamber remained completely empty.

No, not quite empty. Images of a confident young warrior from Dathomir filled Jaina's vision: Tenel Ka raising her cup in a pledge of friendship, Tenel Ka braiding her long hair in preparation for Jedi training exercises, Tenel Ka scaling the outer walls of the Great Temple, pulling herself up easily hand-over-hand. Jaina could sense through their connection in the Force that similar thoughts troubled her twin brother.

Just moments after Jaina took a seat near Jacen, the Jedi historian and instructor Tionne appeared through a side door and came to stand near the three trainees. Jaina felt her brother's mood brighten at the sight of the silvery-haired Jedi woman. Tionne had taught them to look for multiple solutions to any problem, to find choices, fresh perspectives, new alternatives. As always, Jaina was struck by the wisdom in the mother-of-pearl eyes, wisdom gained from years of studying the tales and lore of ancient Jedi.

Tionne's voice was soft and melodious. "Master Skywalker has asked me to . . . help you to move forward in your lightsaber training."

Jaina shifted uncomfortably, not wanting to think about the deadly weapon she wore clipped to a utility loop on her orange jumpsuit.

Tionne motioned to the three seated trainees. "Please. Come up on the platform where we have more room to work."

Jacen and Lowie mounted the steps, but Jaina hung back, not sure if she could express her reluctance. But when Tionne beckoned again, smiling at her with kind patience, Jaina found herself moving to join the others.

With each step, her lightsaber bumped against her leg, a grim reminder of its deadly presence. Her heart began to pound with dread, and a cold sweat broke out on her neck and forehead. Continuing with her lightsaber training, she could see now, was going to be even more difficult than she had expected, and Jaina could tell from the set of

Jacen's jaw that her brother was also struggling to control his own anxiety. He must have sensed her difficulty too, because he turned to her with a shaky smile. "Want to hear a joke?"

She forced a laugh. "Why not?"

This took her brother by surprise, and he paused a moment to think. "Okay, why is a droid mechanic never lonely?"

Jaina shrugged, knowing better than to attempt an answer.

"Because he's always making new friends!"

Jaina giggled in spite of herself, grateful for the release in tension. Lowie let loose a bark of laughter as well. A dimple appeared in Tionne's cheek, and the approving glow in her alien eyes showed that she understood how hard this must be for all of them.

Then, spacing the trainees two meters apart, each facing the same direction, Tionne took them through a series of exercises, using only the hilts of their lightsabers. Clearing her mind of all else, Jaina echoed the instructor's strong, fluid movements as if she were performing a dance.

Apparently satisfied with their progress, Tionne ended the exercise and came to stand in front of Lowie. Gesturing for Jaina to take a position beside her, facing Jacen, Tionne pressed a stud on the handle of her weapon and a shimmering silver beam sprang from it, coruscating with energy.

"Please ignite your lightsabers," she said.

Though a frown of doubt crossed Jacen's face, he soon held a glowing emerald blade. With a snap-hiss, Lowie's blade appeared too, blazing a deep gold, like molten bronze. He held it at his side.

"Oh, *do* be careful, Master Lowbacca," Em Teedee said from the Wookiee's waist. "You know how delicate my circuitry is."

Biting her lower lip, Jaina closed her eyes and touched a button on her lightsaber. Her weapon whooshed to life; the flare of its electric-violet beam and the light of the three other energy blades penetrated even through her shut eyelids, bringing with them a flood of vivid memories.

Violet. The color of the evil Nightsister Tamith Kai's eyes.

Silver. Brakiss's flowing robes. The Shadow Academy. Jacen and Jaina dueling with each other in holographic disguise. A mistake by either of them could have meant death.

Bronze. Almost the reddish gold of Tenel Ka's hair. Tenel Ka's severed arm, still holding the handle of the failed lightsaber as it exploded. The shock on Tenel Ka's face as an emerald blade sliced through her arm.

Emerald green. The color of Zekk's eyes, sur-rounded by a dark corona. Zekk, who was even now being trained on the Shadow Academy, learning to serve the Second Imperium and using the dark side of the Force. And if the Second Imperium attacked the New Republic as planned—the New Republic that Jaina and Jacen and Luke Skywalker's other Jedi Knights had sworn to protect—she would be forced to fight. How could she not defend the New Republic, when her mother was its leader?

Would she have to face Zekk with a lightsaber to protect her own mother?

With a cry, Jaina switched off her weapon and dropped it to the flagstones, backing away from it as if it had turned into a krayt dragon. An instant later all lightsabers were extinguished, and Jaina shuddered with relief.

Tionne's pearly eyes were grave as she looked at her three young charges. Picking up Jaina's discarded lightsaber, she seated herself on the cool stone of the raised platform and said, "Please, make yourselves comfortable. I need to tell you a story."

Jaina, Jacen, and Lowie settled in a tight half-circle around her, crowding close, needing the contact. Tionne sat straighter and held her delicate hands before her, moving them as she wove her tale like an invisible tapestry before their eyes.

"Thousands of years ago, in a time of great evil and great good," Tionne began in her rich musical voice, "there lived a woman named Nomi Sunrider with her husband Andur, who was training to be a Jedi Knight.

"When Nomi and her husband traveled to take a

gift of precious Adegan crystals to Andur's new Jedi Master, they were stopped by a group of greedy bandits, who killed Nomi's husband and tried to steal the crystals. But when Nomi saw her husband lying dead, she snatched up his lightsaber and took a deadly revenge on his murderers. Afterward, seeing what she had done, Nomi was so filled with revulsion that she vowed never to touch a lightsaber again.

"To fulfill the dying wish of her husband, Nomi carried the crystals to his Jedi Master, Thon. There she stayed with her baby daughter Vima and began her own training to become a Jedi. She learned and grew in wisdom and the Force, but still she refused to touch a lightsaber, although it was the weapon of the Jedi.

"Eventually, however, there came a day when she discovered that her power with the Force alone could not protect the ones she loved. To save her beloved Jedi Master and to guard her daughter, Nomi once again took up a lightsaber and fought for what she knew was right.

"But by this time Nomi understood the purpose and meaning of the lightsaber—and from that day forward she fought with all the power of the light side of the Force. She was never eager to use her lightsaber, but she knew it was occasionally necessary. By learning to accept this, she became a great Jedi Master and a great warrior."

As the story ended, Jaina drew a deep refreshing breath, coming out of the near trance she entered whenever listening to Tionne's tales. Jaina sensed that much of the horror she had felt earlier had already drained away, though her muscles were as sore and weary as if she herself had fought all of Nomi Sunrider's lightsaber battles.

Jaina felt something heavy and solid slide into her hand. She glanced down to see the handle of her lightsaber. Tionne had slipped it to her.

"No need to turn it on for now," the Jedi instructor said gently, looking directly into Jaina's brown eyes. "I think we've come far enough for today."

10

DOCTORS WERE BORN meddlers, Tenel Ka decided with annoyance.

The fifth court physician in as many hours continued explaining in a calm, patronizing voice that, although Tenel Ka was perfectly correct in not desiring a crude droid arm, she could have *no* objection to a lifelike biomechanical prosthetic replacement. (Apparently they thought they knew her better than she knew herself.) Tenel Ka finally raised the stump of her arm in exasperated surrender and let the doctor have her way. The physician looked satisfied and not at all surprised that Tenel Ka had agreed. After all, it had been the only reasonable choice.

The doctor beckoned to one of her nurses, and the man came forward to begin taking measurements of the stump of Tenel Ka's left arm. Next, an engineer placed electrodes against her scarred skin and sent intermittent jolts of electricity into the flesh—to measure the nerve conduction, she explained.

Meanwhile, the nurse placed Tenel Ka's right arm

in a holographic imaging chamber. Each time the engineer administered a jolt to Tenel Ka's stump, the nurse patted her shoulder comfortingly and asked her to hold still. The man took great pride in telling her how the holographic image would be reversed to make a pattern that could be used as the mold for her new biosynthetic left arm.

Like children let loose at a sweets bazaar, physicians buzzed around the room snapping orders, conferring with each other, and making preparations. Allowing the poking and prodding and the chaos of voices to fade into the background, Tenel Ka sank into her own thoughts.

As the daughter of two strong ruling families, one from Hapes and one from Dathomir, Tenel Ka had long known who and what she was. Her philosophy of life had been as clear in her mind as her views on lineage, loyalty, friendships, and even her own physical abilities and limitations.

If one of those components changed, did everything else change as well?

From childhood, Tenel Ka's parents had taught her to make her own decisions based in equal part on reason, fact, and personal belief. Therefore, she had never been one to sit passively while others made choices for her. Yet, since the loss of her arm, hadn't she done just that?

She had hardly given it a thought when Ambassador Yfra appeared in the middle of the night to whisk her away from Yavin 4 in secret. In these last few days on Hapes, Tenel Ka had allowed her grandmother to control her movements and communications, tell her when to sleep, bring all her meals, and select appropriate clothing for her. And now Tenel Ka, who had always relied on her own mind and body, was allowing herself to be fitted for a biomechanical arm.

Had she truly changed so much?

The Force was a part of her, flowing through her just as the blood of her parents flowed through her veins. But this artificial arm was no part of her. If she accepted it, then she was allowing the loss of her limb to change her in ways that reached deeper than the eye could see. She didn't object to changing—but this change was not for the better. If she allowed herself to be transformed, it should be in the direction of becoming stronger or wiser.

Tenel Ka's reverie was cut short by the sound of whirring servomotors. The doctor and an engineer stood before her holding a grotesque metallic arm. A droid arm. It reminded Tenel Ka of the unwieldly contraption she had heard the former TIE pilot Qorl now wore since going back to serve the Second Imperium. Tenel Ka shook her head in wordless denial.

"Now this is only temporary, of course," the doctor said with the same infuriating condescension she had used before. "Just accustom yourself to it while we're synthesizing the biomechanical arm."

Tenel Ka decided then and there that she had not, in fact, changed that much. If she needed to use the Force from now on to assist her in small ways, then so be it. But she refused to become dependent on a machine that masqueraded as part of herself.

"No," she managed to croak when the doctor moved to attach the mechanical arm to her severed limb. The engineer backed away uneasily, but the doctor continued as if Tenel Ka had not spoken.

"This is all part of the process of making you whole again," the doctor said in her maddening voice, "and that is exactly what you want."

"No," Tenel Ka repeated, setting her jaw stubbornly. Anger seethed inside her at the doctor's confident presumption that she knew what was best.

The doctor shook her head and bent down, as if chiding a young child. "Now, you agreed to be fitted for this new arm and—"

"I've changed my mind," Tenel Ka gritted, clamping down on her temper to hold it in check.

The doctor's lips were still smiling, but grim determination shone in her eyes, indicating she would never take no for an answer—not from any patient of *hers*. The woman kept up a steady stream of talk and motioned for the engineer to help her position the droid prosthetic against the stump of Tenel Ka's arm, as if the doctor thought that by forging ahead she could overwhelm her patient's determination with her own.

"Now, there's no disgrace in having a biomechanical arm, you know. Even your great Jedi Master Skywalker has a prosthetic hand."

Tenel Ka acknowledged inwardly that there had been no weakness in Master Skywalker's choice. It made him no more or less than what he was. He had wrestled with his own decisions and made his own choices, just as she must make hers. The Jedi Master would not ask her to do otherwise—as the people who surrounded her here on Hapes seemed intent on doing.

"Your new arm will look quite natural," the doctor went on in her exasperating, soothing voice, "and your grandmother has spared no expense."

When the cold metal of the mechanical limb touched Tenel Ka's arm, she lost the last vestiges of control over her anger.

"No!" Tenel Ka cried, unconsciously using the Force to give the engineer and the doctor a backward shove. The droid arm was already clamped in place against her skin, however, like a protruding cancerous growth.

"I said NO!" Tenel Ka quite consciously used the Force to yank the contraption free and fling it with blinding speed against the nearest wall. It hit the stones with a clang and a crunch and fell in pieces to the cold tile floor.

Gasps went up from all around the room, and a dozen pairs of eyes regarded her with shock and apprehension.

Having vented her fury, Tenel Ka's voice was now quite calm. "And I meant no."

11

THE BUZZING VIBRATION of the T-23 skyhopper both soothed and unsettled Jacen for some reason he could not define.

Up in the cockpit with Lowie, Em Teedee amplified his speaker volume to be heard above the whine of the engines. "Really, Master Lowbacca, I don't see what the point of all this flying about could be, without even so much as a destination in mind."

At Lowie's soft growl, the little droid replied, "Therapeutic? For what? And in any case, I should think that performing some sort of physical exercise would be far more beneficial than flying aimlessly over the treetops."

Jaina sat pensively beside Jacen in the skyhopper's cramped passenger seat, toying with her lightsaber. "We actually tried that, Em Teedee, but lately it seems like any exercise we do only reminds us of the things we were trying to get our minds off of in the first place."

Jacen was surprised to hear Jaina answering the

pesky little droid just as Lowie had addressed it a moment earlier—without annoyance, and as a friend. In fact, a full day had passed since any of them had had the heart to switch Em Teedee off. It was as if they hoped the little translator's chatter might fill the void that none of them wished to think about.

But something *was* missing, Jacen thought. Different. Under normal circumstances he probably would have been crowded into the tiny cargo well behind the passenger seat . . . and he would have happily endured that discomfort, if it meant that Tenel Ka could have been with them, sitting where he now sat.

"Oh, dear me!" Em Teedee said in a much subdued voice. "How terribly insensitive my processor can be. You've all been thinking of Mistress Tenel Ka, haven't you? I *am* dreadfully sorry."

Jacen saw Lowie reach down to give the little droid what looked like a comforting pat. Now that Em Teedee had brought up the subject the friends had been avoiding, Jacen felt Tenel Ka's absence all the more keenly.

"It's okay, Em Teedee," Jaina said. "We all miss her."

Jacen sighed. "I wish I could just talk to her."

Jacen, Lowie, and Em Teedee voiced agreement. Then, as though they had discussed it and come to a unanimous decision, Lowie turned the T-23 about and headed back to the Jedi academy.

*   *   *

Master Luke Skywalker looked down at his small barrel-shaped astromech droid as they entered the hangar bay at the base of the Great Temple. "I'm fine, Artoo," he said, answering the droid's questioning whistle. "I just have an important decision to make."

Luke frowned and thought back on the direct communication he had just sent to the Fountain Palace on Hapes. He had been unable to get hold of Prince Isolder and Teneniel Djo, Tenel Ka's parents. Instead, Ta'a Chume, the matriarch of the Royal House, had come onscreen and told him in no uncertain terms that Tenel Ka's parents were traveling outside the Hapes Cluster and could not be reached, and that the princess herself had already endured enough trauma because of her Jedi training. Under no circumstances would the young woman be allowed to speak with Master Skywalker. With that, the former queen had abruptly terminated the connection, leaving Luke with an entirely new set of concerns.

Tenel Ka's grandmother had never approved of the direction the girl had chosen for her own life. The harsh old woman had always wanted to mold her granddaughter into a scheming politician of whom she could be proud—someone just like herself.

What if, Luke wondered, instead of supporting

and comforting Tenel Ka during this time of turbulence, her grandmother chose to use Tenel Ka's
weakness to her own advantage? Without Isolder
and Teneniel Djo to support their daughter emotion-
ally, Tenel Ka might be too despondent or confused
to make her own choices. It was possible she would
blindly accept any decision the matriarch might
make on her behalf.

Luke shook his head. Political considerations
aside, Tenel Ka would not find the comfort she
needed from her grandmother. He thought of the
close bond the four young Jedi Knights had devel-
oped from working and training together at the
academy. Tenel Ka needed that kind of closeness
right now. She needed the unselfish caring that
Jacen, Jaina, and Lowie could provide.

Luke had no wish to influence Tenel Ka's decision about whether or not to return to Yavin 4; that
would have to be her choice, and hers alone. And
certainly any competent medical droid could be
trusted to tend Tenel Ka's physical wound. But she
needed the warmth and support of friends in order
to heal her emotional wounds and come to her own
decision.

Luke smiled as he saw Lowbacca maneuver the
T-23 skyhopper onto its pad in the hangar bay.
Those Jedi trainees needed to have their emotional
wounds healed as well. He straightened and walked
toward the T-23. "I think we'd better do a preflight

check on the *Shadow Chaser,* Artoo. Let's get ready to fly."

Artoo warbled and beeped, asking a question.

"Yes," Luke Skywalker said. "I've made my decision."

From the moment her uncle announced he would take them to see Tenel Ka after all, adrenaline began to rush through Jaina's veins. She made a mad dash for her chambers, snatched a fresh jumpsuit, a Jedi robe, and a few other odds and ends, then stuffed them along with her lightsaber into a small flight duffel. By the time she raced back out of her quarters, down the echoing stone stairs and hallways, and out onto the landing pad, where their ship waited, she no longer had any idea what she had packed.

Jacen arrived ahead of her, running up the ramp of the sleek *Shadow Chaser,* a disordered pile of clean clothes tucked under one arm, his lightsaber under the other. Jaina didn't slow as she followed him up the ramp, marveling as she always did at the powerful ship and its glossy quantum armor. The ship had once been the finest craft created by the Second Imperium. After Master Luke Skywalker and Tenel Ka had used it to rescue the twins and Lowie from the Shadow Academy, the New Republic had given the *Shadow Chaser* to the Jedi Master for his own use.

Once Lowie had scrambled aboard with Em Teedee, his lightsaber clipped to the webbed belt at his waist, Luke instructed Artoo-Detoo to raise the boarding ramp, and the *Shadow Chaser* lifted off.

Jaina felt a thrill as the *Shadow Chaser*'s repulsorlifts boosted them off the landing field; sublight engines kicked in, launching them away from the jungle moon. The last few minutes of rushed preparation were a blur in her mind, and she looked around for something else to speed them on their way.

Lowie rumbled a question from the navigation console, and Em Teedee answered, "No, I'm certain Master Luke doesn't need our assistance in plotting the most efficient route."

Her uncle smiled down at the Wookiee. "We'll be going to lightspeed in just a few minutes. Why don't you all try to relax, get some rest."

Jaina took a deep breath and watched the stars through the viewports—like glittering gems sinking in a depthless black sea—until each pinprick of light elongated into a starline and the *Shadow Chaser* made a smooth jump into hyperspace.

The three Jedi trainees found they were too excited to rest, though. They spent the remainder of the journey trying to distract themselves aboard the tiny ship. Jaina and Lowie were just about to remove an access panel to the rear thruster stabilizers to study how they worked when Luke announced their final approach to Tenel Ka's home planet.

The three friends rushed to the cockpit. As they took their seats behind the Jedi Master, Lowie squinted and scanned the star system around them. When she saw his ginger-furred face register surprise, Jaina looked around, seeing no nearby planet that could have been Dathomir.

"That's odd," she said at last. "From the descriptions I've heard and the star charts I've studied, I could swear we were in the Hapes Cluster."

Her uncle swiveled in the pilot seat and met each pair of eyes in turn.

"We *are* in the Hapes system," Luke said gravely. "It's time I explained to you that Tenel Ka is more than just a simple warrior from a backward planet."

12

BROAD-SHOULDERED NORYS, former leader of the Lost Ones gang and new stormtrooper trainee, spread his white armor on the bunk in front of him. He studied the pieces carefully, then began to assemble the glossy outfit, donning the components one at a time—and enjoying every minute of it.

The boots went on first, stiff and sturdy. Then the greaves, the shin armor, the leg plates, body armor, arm plates, and finally the flexible but tough gloves. He felt as if he had been transplanted into the body of an assassin droid, a fighting machine encased in an impenetrable shell.

Norys allowed himself a satisfied smile. This was much more impressive than anything his gang members had ever scrounged deep in the decaying alleys of Coruscant's underworld. He had been the toughest, meanest, angriest young brute of all the gang members. But being a stormtrooper was better . . . so much better.

All of his former companions were also soldier

recruits undergoing training. Norys fully expected to be the best among the new troops, just as he had been toughest among the Lost Ones.

On the downside, he was no longer his own boss, free to do as he wished. He had to follow the orders of the Second Imperium. But with armor such as this and the military might of those who followed their Emperor, it was all worth it. Besides, if Norys proved himself valuable enough, his rank would increase, and he'd be placed in command of more soldiers, maybe even fly a TIE fighter. Without a doubt, he would have more power and cause much more damage than he'd ever imagined when he was just a gang leader.

Things were looking up.

The last piece of his stormtrooper outfit was the hard white helmet with black eye goggles and mouth speakers. He slipped the helmet over his head and locked it into place at the neck joint. At last he stood totally encased, completely protected—no longer a disreputable bully with a grimy outfit and stolen scraps as his only possessions.

Now he was someone to be reckoned with: a *stormtrooper*.

Norys marched down the corridor, taking care to clomp loudly on the deck plates with his armored boots. They made such a satisfying sound.

He had memorized the layout of the Shadow

Academy station and knew exactly how to get to the private training room where old Qorl, the former TIE pilot, had ordered him to report. Standing outside the sealed door, he keyed in the access code—he'd felt a private thrill when Qorl had given him the secret numbers—and waited for the computer to process his entry request.

With a hiss like an angry serpent, the door slid aside. Norys marched boldly into the shielded room, and the door sealed itself behind him.

Qorl stood inside the training chamber holding a wicked-looking spear in his black-wrapped left hand. His droid replacement arm gripped the gleaming shaft with enough force to dent the metal. The serrated head of the spear had a long central prong with two side spikes curving up like a dragon's barbed tail.

"You're late," Qorl said. He cocked his droid arm back—and hurled the deadly weapon at Norys with all the strength in his robotic servomotors!

Norys stood astonished as the deadly spearpoint hurtled toward his chest plate. He just had time to cry "Hey!" in a panicked voice amplified by his helmet speakers before the barbed tip impacted squarely with enough force to smash him backward.

Norys slammed into the wall, his helmet ringing against the hard metal bulkhead. His vision sparkled with impending unconsciousness. He expected to see a spear sprouting from his heart and waited for his nerves to send shouts of mortal pain. He wanted to scream that Qorl, his supposed teacher, had betrayed him, murdered him—

But a split second later his thoughts cleared enough to hear the clatter as the spear shaft fell harmlessly to the floor. He looked down at his chest in amazement and saw only a nick in the white armor where the spear had struck.

"What did you do that for?" Norys shouted.

Qorl answered in a gruff but calm voice. "To teach you respect for your stormtrooper armor, Norys," he said, "but also to warn you not to become overconfident. Yes, that armor is powerful enough to stop many weapons, such as this crude spear." The TIE pilot nodded toward the jagged weapon on the floor plates.

Norys bent down to grab the spear, narrowing his eyes in rage as he looked at his teacher. The old pilot had made a fool out of him. He felt a dangerous anger boiling through his veins. He had a good mind to take the triple-pronged spear and attack the pompous old man with it.

"But don't think your armor is invincible." Qorl reached inside his uniform, pulled out a deadly blaster pistol, and pointed it directly at Norys. "For instance, this blaster could slice through that armor as if you were wearing nothing at all."

Norys stiffened, looking into the ominous snub barrel of the pistol. His mind raced. What had he gotten himself into? Why was Qorl so upset with him? He wondered whether he could swing the spear, knock the blaster away, and strike down the TIE pilot. That would serve the old man right. . . .

Qorl turned the blaster pistol around and extended it toward Norys, butt end first. "Here. This will be your personal weapon," he said.

Norys dropped the spear to the floor and tentatively took the blaster. The pistol felt very good in his gloved grip. Qorl nodded at him. "For target practice," he said, then went over to the controls by the door.

The gray light-absorbing walls of the windowless room shimmered.

Suddenly Norys found himself standing in a dank, dim cave with fanged stalactites dripping from the walls and ceiling. Long spikes of stalagmites rose like blunt knives from the floor. Unseen water trickled somewhere, and a pallid light seemed to ooze from the pale rock itself. Despite the room's visible transformation, Norys could detect no change in the smell of the air through his helmet filters.

"The walls of this chamber will absorb blaster bolts," Qorl said. "Your weapon has already been set to full power. There won't be much recoil, but you must become accustomed to how it feels to aim and shoot and hit a target. Pay attention now. Watch for them as they attack."

"Watch for what?" Norys said, looking around from right to left. "What's going to attack me?"

The cave seemed more sinister now. The eye goggles distorted his vision, and he tried to compensate. Strange creature noises burbled and hummed from every direction. He couldn't tell if they were insects or rodents, but they sounded vicious to him, as if everything within this chamber might be a predator.

Norys had hunted in the lower alleys of Coruscant, tracking giant granite slugs, multifanged spider-roaches, mutated feral rats—and his intuition told him this was simply a testing chamber on the Shadow Academy. He didn't think there could be any real danger. Not really.

However, this cave certainly seemed real enough. . . .

With a squalling cry, a leathery-winged creature dropped out of its hiding place in the ceiling and swooped toward him. Its eyes were huge and slitted, and Norys could see pointy ears or antennae on top of its head and razor claws at the ends of its flapping wings as it swept down.

A mynock. They weren't supposed to be terrible predators—but from the wicked fangs and claws as it swooped toward him, Norys decided this was one mynock with a bad attitude.

He pointed the blaster and squeezed off an energy bolt, but the beam went wide, striking a stalactite and startling up four more of the angry flying creatures. The new batch of mynocks also attacked, annoyed at him for disturbing their dark slumber.

Norys squeezed the firing button again and again, adjusting his aim as he watched the bright bolts streak through the dimness. The brilliant spears of light dazzled his eyes, and he could barely see through his filtered goggles.

The devilish mynocks swooped and avoided the deadly beams.

This wasn't fair! It was supposed to be target practice. He should have been able to point at a bantha's-eye or hide behind a window while shooting at an unsuspecting target in the streets below, as he had often done on Coruscant.

The blaster missed again and again as mynocks swirled around him, flapping their wings and assailing his ears with skull-splitting screeches. Norys wondered if Qorl had intentionally adjusted the blaster's aimpoint to throw the beam off.

He suddenly realized that he had been aiming wrong. It was his own fault. Reacting wildly to his sudden fear, he had overcompensated.

As the first mynock came toward him again, claws outstretched and long fangs ready to tear him to shreds, he took a second to aim and squeezed off a long bolt that sizzled through the creature's body. The mynock gurgled and fell to the floor, where it was impaled by one of the stalagmites.

"Yes!" Norys shouted in triumph—but three new mynocks swirled around him, attracted by his shout. He fired again and missed. The creatures came at him from the front, side, and behind. Norys turned, remembering to *think*, point, aim, and shoot. He eliminated another creature.

Two more emerged from the ceiling, but Norys swiveled at the waist and forced himself to concentrate. One of the two struck from behind, though its claws skittered off Norys's white stormtrooper armor. He ignored it as he set the second mynock firmly in his sights and shot it.

"Gotcha!" He turned and carefully targeted the remaining creatures, one after another. Gradually, his shooting improved. He learned how to aim. He had learned how to be deadly.

Finally, his blaster pack winking from low charge, Norys stood still and waited—but no more of the creatures emerged from the illusionary cave. He squinted through his goggles, alert for a new attack.

The walls of the cave shimmered and vanished, leaving only the flat metal shell of the training chamber. He allowed himself to relax.

"Good," Qorl said.

Norys turned to see the old TIE pilot standing next to the controls. In the excitement of the exercise, he had forgotten entirely about the military instructor.

"That was fun," Norys said. "I'm getting good at it." He looked down at the blaster, wondering when he'd be able to use it next, when he'd be allowed to practice against a real target.

"You did well enough, Norys," Qorl said again, "but you must remember—*mynocks don't shoot back.*"

Qorl pushed another button on the controls, and the door to the training chamber opened. "Come, we must go to the assembly rooms. Everyone will be there." The old TIE pilot waited for Norys to march ahead of him. "Our Great Leader is planning to address the Shadow Academy"

Zekk sat smothered in his private shell of self-confidence as dozens of Dark Jedi students gathered in the confined room where Master Brakiss and Tamith Kai lectured them in the ways of the dark side.

Zekk wore his padded suit of dark leather armor and sat straight and proud, shoulders squared. His lightsaber hung comfortably at his side. After weeks of training, he had grown fully comfortable with it. It was like a part of him, an extension of his body. That, more than anything else, convinced him he was destined to be a Jedi Knight. He was a loner, but he was also the most powerful of Brakiss's students. The other trainees flashed him occasional glances. Zekk had rapidly surpassed all of them, even those who had been at the Shadow Academy for months and months.

But then, Zekk had the greatest motivation. He wanted to be strong. He wanted everything the Force could give him.

Among those gathered in the assembly hall he noticed Vilas, the Nightsister Tamith Kai's dark-haired and brooding trainee. Vilas, who was from Dathomir, was arrogant and smug, always looking down at him, never letting him forget that it was *he* who had stunned Zekk when he'd resisted capture on Coruscant. Zekk wasn't about to forget. He felt a rivalry with this swarthy young man who talked too often about how he had ridden rancors and summoned storms on Dathomir—as if Zekk was supposed to be impressed.

The ominous Tamith Kai stood next to her protégé Vilas. She and the new Nightsisters had begun training Vilas during the Shadow Academy's construction. They therefore considered him the first of the new Dark Jedi, stronger than the others. For now.

Zekk crossed his arms over his leather-armored chest, knowing that they were wrong. And one day, Zekk told himself, he would prove it.

Burly Norys and the Lost Ones—new storm-trooper recruits taken under the wing of military commander Qorl—stood at attention. The other senior-ranking stormtroopers seemed at ease, while the Lost Ones appeared restless and uncomfortable in their new body armor.

But everyone listened intently to the Great Leader's speech.

In the center of the chamber the overwhelming and awesome image of the Emperor Palpatine filled the open space in the confined room. The glowing hologram towered taller than any person present, a paternal figure and stern watchman.

Crackling from transmission static, the image of the cowled Emperor addressed them from his hideout somewhere in the Core Systems. Yellow reptilian eyes under hooded brows watched the gathered students. The eye of Palpatine was always on them.

"Our plans for the Second Imperium are close to completion," the Emperor said. "All beings are doing their part to return a New Order to our galaxy. Each of you will help my Second Imperium become powerful. Each of you is an important part of a great machine that will crush the Rebellion and put an end to their so-called New Republic."

The holographic image pivoted, giving the impression that Palpatine's gaze was sweeping across each and every person there.

"Our space fleet grows day by day, thanks to the hyperdrive cores and turbolaser batteries stolen in a recent brilliant military ambush. That equipment is helping us create our own battle fleet. Our ships will at first be smaller than the behemoths the New

Republic can bring against us—but we shall fight, and we shall win. Our army of Dark Jedi is nearly complete."

The Emperor seemed to grow larger, his image swelling to loom above them. The rippling hood around Palpatine's shriveled face seemed to blow in an unseen wind. His eyes widened, blazing with the light of twin white suns.

The Emperor's voice boomed out, raised to such a volume that Zekk flinched. "Hear me, my Jedi Knights and stormtroopers. The Force does not favor weaklings. *We* have the strength. The Force is with *us*—to victory!"

Then the transmission ended, and the Emperor's cowled silhouette dissolved into sparkles and static.

The entire assembly set up a deafening cheer, in which Zekk joined wholeheartedly.

13

FLANKED BY A pair of Hapan Stinger security escort vehicles, the *Shadow Chaser* touched down lightly on the main landing pad of the Fountain Palace. In the cockpit, Luke Skywalker gave a small sigh of relief. Letting his eyes fall closed for a moment, he reached deep within himself, found the calm core of Force at his center, and then focused outward.

Artoo-Detoo gave a short warble, and Luke opened his eyes to find all three young Jedi Knights already unbuckled from their crash webbing and scrambling toward the exit hatch, barely able to restrain their impatience. Jacen bounced nervously from one foot to another, while Lowie raked fingers through his ginger fur in an effort to smooth it down. Jaina shrugged and looked at him. "Well, what are we waiting for, Uncle Luke?"

Chuckling, Luke released the flight interlocks, and the three Jedi trainees tumbled down the ramp as soon as it began to extend. Ta'a Chume, in the customary half-veil she wore for public appearances, was already waiting on the landing pad with a retinue of guards and attendants. Luke was pleased to see the twins and Lowie greet the old matriarch with courtesy and respect.

The former queen looked coldly at Luke as he began his greeting. "I'm sorry, but your journey here has been a complete waste, Jedi Master. You see, my granddaughter will not be able to speak with—"

Just then Jaina gave a delighted cry, and Jacen yelled, "Hey, Tenel Ka, are we ever glad to see you!" Lowie bellowed a loud Wookiee greeting. The three young visitors rushed across the landing platform to embrace their friend, who had emerged from the sparkling palace. Snatches of the excited conversation drifted to where Luke stood.

"Master Lowbacca wishes to compliment you on how, er, well-rested you look."

"Thought we'd never see you again."

"I am glad you came."

"Want to hear a joke?"

Luke's attention was drawn back to Ta'a Chume when she spoke to her nearest attendant. "I didn't call the princess. How could she possibly—"

"I called to her," Luke said simply.

Ta'a Chume shook her head. "Impossible. We would have picked up any transmission from your ship."

Luke allowed himself the barest smile at her

mystification. "I didn't use a transmitter," he said. "I called her through the Force. You may wish it weren't true, but Tenel Ka is already more Jedi than you know."

The matriarch raised her brows, but her eyes were unreadable. "We shall see, Jedi Master. The princess may yet get over that foolish notion."

"Does it matter to you what your granddaughter wants for herself?" Luke asked bluntly. "I know it matters to her parents. When I let her leave my protection on Yavin 4 to return to Hapes, I thought her parents would be here for her. But maybe I shouldn't have sent her away so quickly. Where are Teneniel Djo and your son Isolder?"

Luke saw indecision cloud the matriarch's eyes, and he sensed that she was trying to decide whether she would be better served by the truth or a lie. At last she said, "Although I no longer rule the Hapes Cluster, I still have my sources of information. I learned that an attempt would be made on the lives of the royal family, so I urged my son and his wife to pay a visit of state to another system—to negotiate a liberalization of our trade agreements. The negotiations called for a royal touch, and so my son and his wife were easily persuaded. No one but myself and my most trusted advisor knew when they left or where they went.

"Tenel Ka's accident was an unexpected complication that, unfortunately, may put her in danger, drawing assassins to her, like piranha beetles swarming toward the scent of blood. The princess will be safer here with me than at your primitive temple. She is no longer any of your business, Jedi."

Luke shook his head, unwilling to back down. "Whether or not she remains my business will be for Tenel Ka to decide, when *she* is ready."

Jacen looked around his assigned room and shook his head in amazement. It had been scarcely two hours since he had learned that Tenel Ka was a genuine princess, heir to the entire Hapes Cluster. He hadn't even adjusted to that idea yet. And now this.

His room was more luxurious than any in the Imperial Palace on Coruscant. Rich, exotic scents filled the air, along with the sounds of trickling water, faint music, and chirping avians. Decorative fountains spattered in every room, every corridor, every courtyard, striking musical water chimes.

This was where Tenel Ka had grown up? He still couldn't believe it. Why hadn't she told any of her friends? Uncle Luke had known, of course, but what possible reason could Tenel Ka have had for hiding the truth from her friends for so long? Jacen didn't understand that any more than he understood her refusal to speak to him after he had injured her with his lightsaber.

He cringed again at the thought of the harm he

had caused his friend. Jacen had no idea how Uncle Luke had ever talked Tenel Ka's sharp-tongued grandmother into allowing the twins and Lowie to stay on Hapes for an entire month. He only knew that at the appointed time Luke would return to pick up three or—he hoped—four young Jedi Knights.

A whole month. He'd have to talk to Tenel Ka about the accident soon, to clear the air. But what would he say? She wasn't the same person he had known on the jungle moon. Not now. But then, she had never been the person he thought she was, had she? A real Hapan princess! What *could* he say to her?

"May I enter?" The voice startled him out of his reverie, and Jacen turned to find Tenel Ka standing at the door to his chambers.

"Sure . . . I mean, um, of course," he said, blinking in surprise. "I was just thinking about you."

Tenel Ka nodded as if she had known this and swept into the room. Dressed in a long wine-colored gown topped by a rich cape in velvety silver-gray, hair flowing freely down her back in loose, golden-red ripples, Tenel Ka looked like a stranger to Jacen. He found himself tongue-tied.

She stared at him for a long moment, as if he too were a creature from some unknown world, but when she spoke it was the same Tenel Ka. "The room—it is acceptable?"

A thousand questions, apologies, and bits of news clamored in Jacen's mind, waiting to be spoken. But all he could manage to say was "Hey, it's a great room. This is an amazing place. All those fountains."

Tenel Ka nodded again. "This is a fact."

Jacen tingled with an odd pleasure at Tenel Ka's old familiar phrase. Looking into her cool gray eyes, Jacen struggled to collect himself and harness his racing thoughts. At last he managed to blurt out, "I'm really sorry I hurt you, Tenel Ka. It was all my fault."

"I was to blame."

"No," Jacen hurried to say, "I was being stupid. I was so busy trying to impress you with my dueling skills that I didn't even notice when your lightsaber blade started to fratz out!"

"This is not a fact," Tenel Ka said, frowning. "My own pride caused the accident. I believed my fighting prowess could compensate for any deficiency of my weapon. I foolishly believed that the quality of the energy blade was insignificant compared with the quality of the warrior. This was also not a fact."

Jacen shook his head. "Even so, it should never have happened. I should have—"

"The responsibility is *mine*," Tenel Ka broke in, stamping one foot adamantly, her face flushed with emotion. As if she suddenly felt too hot, she unclasped her cloak and tossed it over the back of a cushioned bench, leaving both of her arms bare.

With a stubborn lift of his chin, Jacen looked at the stump of her left arm. It made him feel sick, and he wanted to turn away. This was the first time he had really seen her injury. "I . . . I won't let you take all the blame. If I'd been letting the Force direct my movements, I would have sensed something was wrong." He pointed to where her arm ended so abruptly. "And *that* would never have happened."

Tenel Ka's eyes flashed with smoky gray fire and, using her right arm to hike up her gown to a comfortable thigh level, she plopped onto the cushioned bench. "And had *I* been using the Force," she argued, "I would already have known my lightsaber blade was inadequate."

"Well, I . . ." Jacen stopped, unable to dredge up a counterargument to convince his infuriatingly proud friend. "I . . ." He cast about furiously for something else to say and finally finished, "Um, want to hear a joke?"

His mouth dropped open in amazement as Tenel Ka burst into peals of laughter. He could tell that this was neither polite amusement nor hysteria, but the laughter of enjoyment that sprang from the heart. It was a wonderful sound—one he had wanted to hear since the first day they met.

"But . . ." Jacen shook his head in confusion. "I didn't even tell my joke."

"Ah," Tenel Ka gasped, and tears of merriment began to stream from her eyes. "Aha. I am so glad you're here."

Jacen shrugged as fresh waves of mirth assailed her. "I'm not objecting, mind you. I just don't get it. What's so funny?"

"We have often been in competition, you and I," she said. "I have missed that. Shall we now compete for the greater share of blame?"

Jacen gave her a lopsided grin. "Nah. I guess all I really need is for you to accept my apology."

Tenel Ka began to object but stopped herself. Her laughter faded and her expression turned sober. As if it took a great deal of effort, she said, "Apology accepted. I . . . forgive you, if that is what you desire." Her last words came out in a whisper: "Jacen, my friend."

Relief rushed through Jacen like a morning breeze clearing remnants of lingering fog. He had been holding his breath, and he nearly choked with emotion at her reply. There were no words to express the flood of feelings that welled up in him, so he sat beside Tenel Ka and put both arms around her.

Tenel Ka returned his hug, as best she could, with both arms. Shaking, she pressed a face wet with tears against his shoulder, and Jacen did not think that they were tears of laughter anymore.

*   *   *

When Tenel Ka and Jacen had both composed themselves, they went in search of Jaina and Lowbacca. Then Tenel Ka took the companions on a whirlwind tour of the Fountain Palace, ending at her own chambers. Because chattering went against her nature, the descriptions she provided were brief and succinct.

When they were alone in her rooms, Tenel Ka showed them her favorite—and most private— place in the Fountain Palace, a completely enclosed terrace garden at the center of her suite of rooms. The three story high ceiling was domed, and could be adjusted to simulate any kind of weather and any time of day or night.

The garden room was fifty meters across, its curved walls decorated with scenes from Dathomir. Terraced planters held bushes and trees, cunningly arranged to look as if they were part of the painted primitive landscapes.

At the middle of the garden, smooth stone benches surrounded a tiny artificial lake. Centered in the crystal-clear water, like a miniature volcano emerging from a primordial sea, stood a peaked island with a real waterfall flowing down one side.

"I come here when my heart is heavy, or whenever I miss my mother's homeworld."

"Beautiful," Jaina whispered.

Warmed by her friend's approval, Tenel Ka took

a seat on one of the stone benches and gestured for the others to join her. "We may speak freely here," she said, "and I will answer your questions."

And so the friends talked, more frankly than they had ever dared before, until Tenel Ka's grandmother arrived to summon them to evening meal.

"The banquet hall is ready," Ta'a Chume announced.

Tenel Ka's jaw took on a stubborn set. For the first time since her return to Hapes, she felt *alive*. How could her grandmother interrupt now? "We would prefer to eat in privacy," Tenel Ka said, knowing that she was displaying an appalling lack of courtly manners. But she didn't care.

The matriarch gave her granddaughter a smug smile. "I've already taken care of that," she said. "I sent away all my attendants and advisors for the evening."

This was an old game that she and her grandmother played—who could outmaneuver whom— and Tenel Ka took up the challenge. "Then it should be no problem if we choose to eat here."

"Oh, but the serving droids have already gone into the banquet hall," the former queen objected. "The meal will be served directly on the hour."

Tenel Ka saw Jaina glance at her chronometer. "But that's only five minutes from now," Jaina said, her eyes registering surprise. "I'll need some time to wash up first."

Lowie grunted his agreement, and Jacen said, "Hey, me too. I think we'd all be a lot more comfortable if we weren't so formal on our first night here." His grin, aimed at Ta'a Chume, was charming and infectious. "And we're all pretty tired from our travels."

Flashing Tenel Ka a look that said she would not give in so easily next time, the matriarch nodded. "Very well, then. I will have the serving droids sent in."

Ta'a Chume withdrew from Tenel Ka's private sanctuary, and they all relaxed, glad of the reprieve. Tenel Ka looked gratefully around at her friends and then said, "Let me show you to the refresher units before our meal arrives." She had just stood up to lead them to the door when suddenly the polished stone shook beneath her feet. An ear-splitting roar rent the air, along with a heavy blast, throwing Tenel Ka to her knees.

Lowbacca yelped with alarm, and Em Teedee replied, "Dear me, yes! Master Lowbacca wishes to inquire as to the origins of all this noise and commotion."

"Yeah," Jacen said, "you didn't warn us you had groundquakes."

Tenel Ka looked back to see the Wookiee scrambling to his feet and helping the twins back up as well. "That was no groundquake," she said, grimly launching herself toward the door. "Come with me."

Tenel Ka's heart raced, though not with exertion, as the four of them pelted down the corridor toward the private dining hall. Thick smoke billowed from the far end of the vaulted passageway. She felt her stomach clench.

Her dread lessened when a pair of guards emerged from the roiling, sooty clouds, supporting her grandmother. Emergency squads rushed to extinguish the fires still blazing inside the dining hall. Ta'a Chume coughed a few times and waved imperiously for the guards to allow her to walk on her own.

"No one hurt," she croaked.

"It was a bomb?" Tenel Ka asked.

Her grandmother motioned them all back the way they had come. "Yes. In the dining hall," she said. "Must leave immediately."

"*We* were all supposed to be in the dining hall!" Jaina blanched. "So that bomb—"

The matriarch nodded. "—was meant for the princess and me."

14

THE ROYAL YACHT, a Hapan Water Dragon, skimmed across the ocean waves at top speed, its repulsorjets kicking up spray. Bright sunlight shone through its transparisteel windowports, and the fresh smell of saltwater and rafts of seaweed filled the air.

Leaning against a windowport, eyes half shut, Tenel Ka watched the water dance and sparkle. She had always thought of Reef Fortress Island as her summer home, a place to enjoy the warm sun, the surf, and the ocean breezes. But in truth, it was a stronghold, a safe haven in time of danger.

"I feel ill," Jaina said. "Mentally and physically."

Tenel Ka, having been lulled by the yacht's rocking movement as it sped across the water, now straightened and blinked in surprise. "What is wrong, Jaina?"

"Do you realize that a few minutes one way or another, and we might all have been blown to bits by that bomb?" Jaina asked incredulously. "Or maybe I'm just a little seasick from these waves."

Tenel Ka looked at each of her friends in turn. Jaina did not look well. Her straight brown hair, dull with perspiration, clung in damp clumps to her pallid face and neck. Lowie, sitting beside Ta'a Chume as she steered the yacht with nonchalant confidence, seemed too interested in the navigational computer to be affected by the waves. Jacen, on the other hand, looked boyishly enthralled by the experience.

Tenel Ka said to Jaina, "You will recover."

Tenel Ka's grandmother spoke from her position at the helm. Although royal guards accompanied them, the former queen preferred to pilot the craft herself. "We're almost to the fortress now. You'll be safe there."

Tenel Ka's eyes narrowed shrewdly as she noted her grandmother's words. "Should you not have said *we* will be safe?"

"You and your friends will be safe, yes," her grandmother said evasively.

"Where will you be?" Tenel Ka asked.

"Much of the time I'll be with you, but I'm not sure I can trust the investigation of this bombing to anyone else. Until I get to the bottom of the plot against us, I may have to travel back and forth between Reef Fortress and the Fountain Palace."

Jaina looked startled. "And leave us on the island alone?"

"You will have a full complement of guards,"

Ta'a Chume said soothingly. "And Ambassador Yfra will stay with you whenever I'm away."

Lowbacca snuffled a question from the navigation station. "Master Lowbacca wishes to inquire whether that island up ahead is our final destination," Em Teedee elaborated.

Jacen and Jaina went to the front windowport to look out at the smear of darkness rising from the sun-dappled water.

"Yes," Tenel Ka's grandmother replied, "that is Reef Fortress."

Tenel Ka didn't move forward to look out at the island. She'd been there so many times, she already knew what she would see. It never changed. She closed her eyes, picturing the rocky spires jutting up from the foamy waters of the ocean. She envisioned the water-level entrance to the cave grotto, the steep stone walls of the fortress itself, the crystal-clear cove where she had once loved to swim, the dizzying heights from the parapets along the impenetrable walls where she could walk or run with the wind in her hair, the gently steaming thermal springs in the cellar that provided fresh water for bathing, cooking, and drinking.

Tenel Ka suddenly realized that she had felt homesick after all for this place that held so many of her happiest memories from her childhood, memories of carefree time spent with her parents. The corners of her mouth turned up slightly. Opening her eyes, she moved to stand beside Jacen. "I can't wait to show you my home."

Although the matriarch offered to select quarters for their guests, Tenel Ka insisted on personally choosing an appropriate room for each of the young Jedi Knights.

Lowbacca's chamber was massive, built at a corner where two of the fortress's protective walls met. The room's appointments were basic, its only decorations an ornamental spear on one of the inner walls and a threadbare tapestry on the other. But through the windows on the two outer walls, the room had a spectacular view of the sheer drop from the stone fortress down to the reef rocks and ocean below. Lowbacca stood by the window casement, staring through the force-field screening with such rapt wonderment on his face that Tenel Ka knew she had chosen well for him.

"Do be careful, Master Lowbacca," Em Teedee squeaked in alarm. "If I were to fall down there, I'm sure the damage to my circuits would be irreparable."

For Jaina, Tenel Ka chose what she had always known as the "gadget room." It had belonged to Tenel Ka's great-grandfather, whose hobby had been inventing and tinkering with machines. Fully half of the chamber was filled with workbenches, adjustable-intensity glowpanels, power droids, electrical implements, and odd-looking equipment in various stages of assembly or disassembly. Jaina stayed behind to investigate the fascinating workshop while Tenel Ka showed Jacen the special room she had picked for him.

When they reached the arched doorway, Tenel Ka found herself assailed by an inexplicable bout of nervousness. What if she had judged wrong for her friend? What if Jacen found this room gloomy or dreary, instead of peaceful and soothing? Oh well, she finally decided, she might as well try for the whole effect.

"I would request," she said uncertainly, "that you close your eyes."

"Sure," Jacen said. "Need to clean it up a bit?" He squeezed his brandy-brown eyes shut.

Tenel Ka opened the door with her right hand and reached out to take his arm with her other—only to remember that she had no left hand. Even though Jacen could not have seen, she felt a flush of embarrassment creep into her cheeks as she grasped his arm with her good hand and led him into the room.

"Uh, if it'll make you more comfortable," Jacen quipped, "I can keep my eyes shut the whole time we're at the fortress."

"That will not be necessary." Tenel Ka shut the door behind her and adjusted the lighting. The room was still dim, but that was unavoidable. "You may look now."

She heard his quick intake of breath, and then a whispered exclamation. "Blaster bolts!"

"It is . . . to your liking?" Tenel Ka moved closer to observe Jacen's expression. In the glow of the violet lighting, his smile flashed a fluorescent white. She noted with great satisfaction the delight that lit his face as he used all of his senses to experience this special room.

Tenel Ka's own sense of wonder was renewed as she looked around with Jacen, as if for the first time. A four-meter-high curved aquarium lined the walls of the circular room, unbroken except for the arched doorway through which they had entered. The air tasted salty and tingled pleasantly in her nostrils. Almost hypnotic in its effect, the bubbling and whishing of recirculating water surrounded them. Colorful creatures of all shapes and sizes propelled themselves through the seawater, lit only by specially regulated glowpanels. Moist tropical warmth wrapped them like a blanket, and Tenel Ka stifled a contented yawn.

Jacen followed suit and then chuckled. "I don't think I'll have any problem sleeping in here," he said. "This is just perfect."

She felt him reach out, grope around for her hand, and then give it a squeeze. Tenel Ka sighed. This room was indeed filled with peace.

After they had had an opportunity to refresh themselves, Tenel Ka took her friends to one of her favorite places on the rocky shore of the island, a tiny cove with calm water in an amazing shade of living green. The four of them waded in the sparkling warm waters, joking and splashing, able to forget for a moment the dangers that had brought them to this place.

Jacen and Jaina wore only the undergarments from their flightsuits, which served admirably as swimming gear as well. Tenel Ka herself had changed into a brief lizard-hide exercise suit and felt more like herself than she had at any time since returning to Hapes.

"If you won't be requiring my services, Master Lowbacca," Em Teedee said, "might I stay on shore and shut down for a rest cycle? I have no idea what saltwater might do to my delicate circuitry."

Tenel Ka watched Lowbacca grumble a reply and splash out of the shallows to place Em Teedee high up on a dry rock. After the Wookiee returned, the four friends waded out toward deeper water, enjoying one another's companionship, along with the feeling of the silky water around them.

When Jacen, Jaina, and Lowie turned onto their backs to float lazily on the surface while they conversed, Tenel Ka absently flipped over and floated as well. In that instant she remembered yet again that one of her arms was missing—but she also realized that, with only a slight adjustment of her posture and weight, she was able to float quite easily. By experimenting, she discovered she could propel herself at surprising speed, using nothing more than her strong legs.

Jacen, who had noticed her tentative attempts, swam over and favored her with what she could only interpret as a challenging grin. Starting to tread water, he raised his eyebrows at her. She met his gaze and began treading water as well—at first with little coordination, then finding her rhythm. When Jacen narrowed his liquid-brown eyes and moved to a sidestroke, Tenel Ka did the same.

Tenel Ka met one challenge after another with varying degrees of success. She found that she was able to do much more than she could ever have imagined. And even when her performance was less than stellar—as when she tried to perform an underwater somersault—she *enjoyed* herself.

When she resurfaced sputtering and coughing after one such attempt, she noticed a measuring look in Jacen's eyes, daring her to push herself to her limits. "Race you to the shore," he said.

Tenel Ka gave him a solemn warning look. "Only if you truly intend to beat me," she said.

Jacen's face was equally grave as he said, "I'll give it everything I've got."

She nodded. "Then—go!"

Tenel Ka drew on all of her strength, endurance, coordination, and ingenuity as she threw her body into the mad race for shore. Her entire consciousness was focused on one goal, and she drove forward with every bit of determination she possessed.

Before she even understood what had happened, she was standing on the shore being greeted by loud cheers from Jaina and a very bedraggled-looking, wet Lowbacca, who were already standing on the rocky beach.

Disoriented, Tenel Ka turned, looking for Jacen, and found him just emerging from the water behind her. From the surprised expression on his face, she knew their competition had been real: he had not "allowed" her to win.

Jaina ran forward to hug them both just as Lowbacca, with a loud Wookiee yell, shook himself dry, sending sprays of salty water in every direction. Jacen yelped, and Jaina gave a small shriek of surprise.

Tenel Ka was glad of the diversion, however, because some of the salty droplets glistening on her face were not seawater.

15

TWO DAYS LATER, the royal matriarch Ta'a Chume looked sternly at her granddaughter as Tenel Ka defiantly tossed aside the embroidered robe of state, as well as the glittering and gaudy tiara.

The former queen was not pleased. "You must dress in a manner befitting your station, child," she said in an indignant tone. "And you might show a bit more respect for your heritage. Take your tiara. It is an heirloom, known throughout the cluster." She held up the delicate crown studded with beautiful, iridescent jewels. "These are rainbow gems of Gallinore, worth enough to buy five solar systems."

"Then buy five solar systems," Tenel Ka said. "I have no use for such wealth."

"You can't avoid your duties by being impertinent. This is not a carefree vacation. There is still work to do. We have an important diplomatic meeting to conduct, and you must prepare yourself."

"I have no interest in your important meeting, Grandmother."

Jacen, Jaina, and Lowbacca stood uncomfortably, not sure what to say as Tenel Ka argued with the matriarch.

"So long as you remain part of the Royal House of Hapes, Tenel Ka, you will continue to receive diplomatic instruction and learn how to become a useful member of our bloodline," her grandmother snapped.

Tenel Ka glared back, her one hand clenched into a fist. "What makes you think I wish to stay here as part of the Royal House? I am still in training as a Jedi Knight."

The matriarch laughed. "Spare me your fantasies, child, and face reality. The Mairan ambassador is on his way to us underwater right now, and we must go meet him at the shore. Put on your robe. I promised him that *you* would be the one to greet him."

"You didn't ask me," Tenel Ka said.

"There was no reason to," the matriarch answered. "You couldn't possibly have other plans, so I just told you."

"I have no need for diplomatic training. I am a fighter, not a politician," Tenel Ka said, indicating with a sweeping gesture the reptile-skin armor she had changed into to emphasize that her preferred heritage was from Dathomir.

"Hey, um, Tenel Ka?" Jacen said uncertainly, clearing his throat. "Uh, I mean, you've got to make up your own mind and everything . . . but remember what Master Skywalker says? Jedi ought to be open to all learning, to draw strength from knowledge—wherever they might find it? Seems to me that even though you're a good fighter, you might someday find a use for the skills your grandmother wants to teach you."

"I disagree with her politics," Tenel Ka said.

Jacen shrugged. "Nobody said you had to do everything the *way* she wants you to."

The matriarch scowled at the insolent young Jedi boy, and that made up Tenel Ka's mind. "Very well. I will do it," she said, "but I will do it my way. This is a fact."

"Oh, excellent!" Em Teedee said from Lowbacca's waist. "Might I take this opportunity to remind you, Mistress Tenel Ka, that a goodly portion of my programming was adapted from protocol droid subroutines? If I can be of any assistance in your political efforts, I gladly offer my services."

The old matriarch looked horrified.

Tenel Ka smiled inwardly. "Thank you, Em Teedee. I accept your offer. Lowbacca, I would like you at my side when I meet the Mairan ambassador."

Tenel Ka picked up the robe and with her one hand attempted to fling it about her shoulders, but the left side slid off, leaving the stump of her arm bare. When the matriarch moved to help her, Tenel Ka pulled away and quickly reached over to tug the garment into place.

"It is good to be an independent thinker, my granddaughter," the matriarch said. "Just have a care you don't do it to excess."

Royal guards had set out a plush chair on the outer edge of the reef, where curling whitecaps chewed against the rock. The damp air smelled of salt and freshness. The old matriarch stood back, observing.

Tenel Ka, in her rippling robe, marched to the chair without waiting for her grandmother to issue instructions. Adjusting the rainbow-gem tiara on her thick red-gold hair, she looked directly into the brisk wind that blew off the choppy waters.

Lowbacca, the breeze ruffling his ginger fur, stood beside Tenel Ka as she seated herself and looked out across the black rocks and the endless sea. She blinked against the bright sunlight and watched the waves for any motion.

The Mairans, a race of intelligent, tentacled, undersea dwellers, came from the ocean world of Maires, one of the planets in the Hapes Cluster. Their ambassadors had set up a consulate on the ocean floor of the Hapes central world. It seemed that, even from their undersea consulate, the Mairan ambassadors had managed to raise a political dispute with their traditional rivals from the planet Vergill.

The Mairans could leave the sea for short periods, but only if the tentacled creatures were periodically showered with a fine spray from bubbling tanks of filtered water they carried on their backs. By keeping their rubbery skin moist, the Mairans were able to spend hours on dry land, and the ambassadors had insisted on coming personally to the island fortress. They would allow the matter to be resolved by no one but the matriarch herself—or a member of the Royal House who was her designee.

The matriarch had designated Tenel Ka.

The princess sat waiting, watching the waves. She had not brought her chronometer along and wondered if the ambassador was late . . . or if she was just impatient for this ordeal to be over with.

Lowbacca stood watch at her side, tall and shaggy; Em Teedee gleamed silver in the sunlight. Jacen and Jaina, who hadn't been briefed, hung back.

"Uh, what are we doing here, exactly?" Jacen asked.

Tenel Ka turned to answer him, but Em Teedee chimed in first. "If I might be permitted to explain, Mistress Tenel Ka? I believe I can provide an appropriate summary." The little droid made a sound as if it were clearing its voice speaker. "Now, then. The Mairan underwater consulate—a domed structure built on their own planet and transported here to the Hapes homeworld—is perilously close to a subsurface mining project opened by the Vergills just after the Mairan consulate was established.

"Although the Vergill mining business is terribly productive, the Mairans have filed a formal complaint because of the noise and the silt stirred up by the drilling and excavation operations. They contend that, since the Mairans were there first, the Vergills should be required to clean up the muddied waters, cease their disruptive mining, and relocate to a place at least fifty kilometers from their consulate."

Tenel Ka nodded. "Yes, these are some of the facts. But not all."

Before she could elaborate, Tenel Ka saw a hulking shape rise out of the water and shamble in her direction, sloshing through the surf. Forty or so black tentacles—which Tenel Ka knew the Mairans let drift free underwater, to grasp any fish that might flit within reach—dangled from its slumped shoulders, and it weaved from side to side on two legs as it walked. The spherical discolored lumps on its sloping head must have been eye membranes. The entire creature looked dark and oily.

Tenel Ka's initial reaction upon seeing the alien

ambassador was one of fear—a giant primeval monster nearly one and a half times her own height rising out of the surf and lumbering toward her— but she pushed the reaction away. Fear could only weaken her judgment right now.

Waves rippled around the Mairan's legs, which were like tree trunks clinging to the beach. Stopping in the low surf, the ambassador held a heavy convoluted shell, into which a pattern of holes had been drilled.

The Mairan ambassador spoke from a vibrating membrane beneath its tentacles in a resonant and burbling voice that was very difficult to understand. *"I am capable of speaking Basic if this is how we must proceed."*

Tenel Ka shook her head. "That will not be necessary. Use your native language." She cast a glance sideways at the silvery ovoid of Em Teedee at Lowie's side. "I have brought my own translating droid."

"Oh, my," said Em Teedee, who just an hour earlier had downloaded the Mairan language from the fortress databanks. "This is quite exciting!"

The tentacled hulk bowed once, then straightened. Placing the drilled side of the shell against its blowhole, it played a skirling, complicated series of flutelike notes.

"Ah, yes," Em Teedee said. "This musical language was indeed properly loaded into my memory banks. Thank the Maker! The Mairan ambassador formally greets you, Princess Tenel Ka."

The tentacled creature blew another series of notes. Em Teedee translated. "And he commends you on your capture of such a magnificent and well-trained pet, with its coat of silky brown seaweed—oh, dear!" the droid chirped. "I do believe he's referring to Master Lowbacca!"

Lowbacca growled and flashed his fangs. Tenel Ka stood, indignant, letting the robe fall away to reveal her reptile-hide armor and her arm stump. Behind them on the rocks, the matriarch frowned in disapproval at her granddaughter's performance.

"Wookiees are an intelligent species. They are *no one's* pets," Tenel Ka said. "This is my friend."

The Mairan appeared flustered, flailed his tentacles in agitation, and played another series of notes. "The ambassador offers his apologies for having misunderstood, Princess Tenel Ka. He grieves for your loss of one . . . tentacle—I believe he means your arm—and hopes that you exacted tenfold retribution on the fool responsible for your loss."

"How I have dealt with the loss of my 'tentacle' is not his concern." Tenel Ka's voice was crisp and hard. "If he has a diplomatic matter to raise, he had better do so immediately. If he tries my patience, I will leave. I have other things to do."

The Mairan ambassador hesitated, its tentacles stirring uncertainly, then raised the shell flute again, drawing forth a long and tangled melody.

"The Mairan ambassador apologizes again and says that he understands the matriarch gave you this decision to make as part of your diplomatic training. Since it is to be your first ruling of major import, you will most assuredly want to give it the utmost time and consideration to choose the best course of action."

Tenel Ka did not back down. Her voice remained stern. "The ambassador is sorely misinformed. I have made *many* important decisions in my life. Although this may be the first one that affects *him* and his kind, he may rest assured that I am no stranger to making tough choices."

Some of those other choices flashed through her mind—particularly her decision to join Master Skywalker's Jedi academy, and her insistence on embracing the Dathomir side of her heritage as well as that of the Hapan Royal House.

"Please present your case without further digression," she said. Her one hand gripped the chair, but she remained standing to minimize the height differential between herself and the towering tentacled ambassador.

"Very well, Princess Tenel Ka Chume Ta' Djo. The Mairan ambassadorial delegation begs the intervention of the Royal House in a matter that has distressed us greatly." Em Teedee had a difficult time keeping up as he translated the fluting notes of the tentacled ambassador's speech.

"Our peaceful undersea settlement is our home on this world, set up by our first delegation no more than six months ago. We have been delighted with the beautiful and tranquil setting of our consulate under the sea. If only you air-breathers could come to see it, I'm certain you would agree that—"

"I'm not a tourist," Tenel Ka said. "What is your grievance?" She already knew, but she wanted him to spell it out.

"Only a month after we established our consulate," the ambassador whistled, "a mining crew of oafish, inconsiderate Vergills set up a floating platform and began drilling less than a kilometer from our settlement structures. The currents are now perpetually stirred up and dirty. The noise vibrates through the water, disturbing our concentration and frightening away fish. They have ruined our home."

The Mairan raised its tentacles beseechingly. "We had established our dwelling there first, most knowledgeable Princess. We beg you to order the despised Vergills to move their pollution away from our home. After all, they have the entire ocean. They need not disturb our peace."

"I understand," Tenel Ka said.

The tentacled ambassador bowed deeply in respect, but then Tenel Ka continued sharply, "I also understand that the Vergills conducted a mining survey of the oceans by satellite, well before you established your consulate city. When I consulted the access records, I learned that you Mairans received a copy of this mining report several months *before* you chose a location for your domed consulate. Finally, I have discovered that you identified the richest vein of ditanium picked up on the survey and chose to place your structure *exactly there,* knowing full well that the Vergills would eventually commence mining operations in the vicinity.

"Yes, Ambassador, the entire ocean *is* available," she said as the wind whipped her hair about like red-gold flames, "but it is you who chose to bring about this dispute. You erected your consulate *after* you knew for certain that the Vergills would desire to mine that very same spot."

She waited, but the Mairan said nothing. She continued. "The Vergills have also petitioned for our intervention. And so you may either change the location of your consulate—which is quite easily done, as I understand from the modular construction of your domes—or you may simply choose to tolerate the noise and disturbance."

After a moment of stung silence, the Mairan ambassador fluted stridently, waving his tentacles. "Don't even bother translating that," Tenel Ka said sharply to Em Teedee, then turned to face the hulking black creature. "You came to me asking for a decision, and I have made it. In the future perhaps you will attempt to work out your own problems instead of wasting our time with your petty squabbles. I have spoken."

She sat back down and shrugged into her robe again. After another moment the Mairan ambassador shuffled backward into the surf and disappeared beneath the waves.

"All right, Tenel Ka!" Jacen cried, running toward her. Lowbacca chuffed with laughter.

Tenel Ka felt her head spinning, exhilarated at what she had done. It surprised her that the speech had come easily after all. She adjusted the rainbow-gem tiara on her head.

She was actually startled, though, when she looked behind her to see her grandmother, the iron-hard and impossible-to-please matriarch, *smiling*.

"Perhaps your methods are a bit rough yet, child," her grandmother said, "but your judgment was sound."

16

REST AND SAFEKEEPING were all well and good, Jacen thought—but after several days staying at the Reef Fortress with no place to go but to the tiny cove to swim, he began to get restless. Terribly restless.

Tenel Ka, too, was a person of action—Jacen knew that better than anybody. She wanted to be out and around, having adventures, not coddled and sheltered like a pet. The injured warrior girl certainly didn't want to sit like an old woman, merely watching waves pound against the rocks.

Ta'a Chume had returned to the Fountain Palace to supervise the investigation of the bomb blast, leaving Tenel Ka and the young Jedi Knights under the questionable care of thin-lipped Ambassador Yfra. The ambassador was a hard woman, as if all the muscles in her body were made of durasteel rather than flesh . . . but then, everyone within the Hapan government lived a harsh life, trusting no one, always struggling for personal gain. Jacen supposed Ambassador Yfra was no worse than anyone else in this society. On the other hand, he could see why Tenel Ka preferred the honest ruggedness of her mother's world of Dathomir to the hypocritical and often poisonous dealings of Hapan politicians.

He found Tenel Ka outside the towering Reef Fortress standing on an outcropping of black rock. She was throwing stones with her good arm into the swirling pools of water that hissed around the outer reef. Deep in concentration, she took careful aim and was clearly pleased whenever she struck her imagined target. Reluctant to disrupt her reverie, Jacen stood behind her, content just to watch.

Jaina and Lowie, who had followed Jacen out of the fortress, also looked on as Tenel Ka threw stones. All of them seemed to feel the same restlessness—stuck on a minuscule island with no place to go.

After a few minutes, the balcony doors above them opened, and a flash of sunlight from polished transparisteel dazzled Jacen. Ambassador Yfra stepped out onto the high balcony, whip-thin, looking like a bird of prey as she scanned the rocks to find them. She waved, catching their attention. "Children, come here please."

Lowbacca sniffed the salty air and groaned a comment. Em Teedee made an electronic sound of disagreement. "I'm sure I don't know what you mean, Master Lowbacca! Whatever makes you think the air has changed for the worse? It still smells every bit as salty and refreshing to *me* as it has for the past hour."

Tenel Ka glanced behind her when Em Teedee spoke and looked momentarily startled to find the others watching her. She clambered off the rock outcropping and joined her three friends. "Let us see what the ambassador wants," she said in a gruff voice, leading the way.

"Maybe it'll be something fun," Jacen suggested.

Tenel Ka looked at him with her granite-gray gaze, raising her eyebrows. "Somehow the ideas of Ambassador Yfra and 'fun' do not go together in my mind."

Jacen snickered at that, wondering if Tenel Ka had purposely made a joke. By all outward appearances she had merely stated a fact.

Inside the fortress, the ambassador met them in the warmly lit balcony room with a surprise for them all. "My dears, I think it's time for you to have a little enjoyment!" she said, smiling with her face, but not with her mind. Jacen could sense it. Although she went through all the correct motions of being friendly and understanding, Jacen could tell that Yfra had no great love for children—or for anyone else who took up so much of her time and interfered with governmental business.

Tenel Ka placed her hand on her hip. "What would you suggest, Ambassador?"

"You children seem so bored," Yfra said. "I can understand that. Sometimes having no cares or worries *is* bothersome." She gave the briefest disapproving frown, then covered it with another false smile. "I've taken the liberty of reprogramming one of our wavespeeders so that you can get away for a while, cruise the ocean, and have a good time out in the sun."

"Are you planning to come along, Ambassador?" Jaina asked.

Yfra made a sour frown, then covered her expression with a cough. "I'm afraid not, young lady. I've terribly important work to attend to. My, you can't imagine the responsibilities I deal with. The Hapes Cluster has sixty-three worlds, with hundreds upon hundreds of different governments and thousands of cultures. Ta'a Chume is a very powerful woman, and we all have so much to do in the absence of Tenel Ka's parents." Yfra clasped her clawlike hands together. "You children ought to enjoy your younger years, while people like me take care of the difficult work."

She shooed them away. "Run along now. Down in the docking bay you'll find the speeder I programmed. It's completely safe, I assure you. I've input a simple loop course that will take you out beyond the reef into the open ocean and then back here by nightfall. I've even seen to it that you have a basket of food, so you can enjoy a meal together while you're out." She drew a deep breath and smiled her insincere smile. "I'm sure you'll have a wonderful time."

Jacen studied the ambassador, trying to determine whether or not to be suspicious. He certainly understood how time-consuming the demands of government could be, since his mother was a Chief of State herself. He also thought of how restless the four companions had been for the past day.

"Blaster bolts! Let's go out and have a good time," he said. "It'll be great to be away from the watching eyes of parents and escorts and ambassadors. I promise you we're going to have fun."

Tenel Ka nodded seriously. "This is a fact." Then she gave him one of the most remarkable gifts Jacen had ever received.

She smiled at him.

The wavespeeder roared across the sea, bouncing and thumping as it crossed the troughs and crests like a wheeled vehicle traveling at high speed across a heavily rutted road. Though the autopilot followed a predetermined course, Jaina and Lowie each took turns at the wheel guiding the rudder, seeing just how far the autopilot would let them deviate from its course. Lowbacca let out a happy-sounding bleat.

Em Teedee said, "Master Lowbacca observes that this vehicle bears some similarity to his own T-23 skyhopper."

Jaina looked at the ginger-furred Wookiee. "Reminds me more of the controls of the *Millennium Falcon*. You and I wouldn't have any problem piloting this thing, Lowie," she said. Lowbacca rumbled in agreement.

The wavespeeder took them away from the rough foamy waters around the reef, on which the isolated fortress towered like a citadel overlooking the blue-green ocean of Hapes.

Jacen sat back and talked with Tenel Ka as they let themselves be lulled by the reflected sunlight and the hypnotic undulation of the waves. "Hey, Tenel Ka," he said tentatively. "I've got a great joke—listen. Which side of an Ewok has the most fur?"

Tenel Ka looked at him seriously. "I have never considered the question."

"The *outside*! Get it?"

"Jacen, why do you so often tell me jokes?" she asked. "I do not believe I ever laugh at them."

Jacen shrugged. "Hey, I was just trying to cheer you up."

Tenel Ka threw him an odd glance. "You think I need cheering up?"

When he answered her, Jacen noticed that he had a difficult time keeping his eyes away from the healed pinkish stump of her arm. "Well, you just seemed kind of quiet and serious."

Tenel Ka raised her eyebrows. "Am I not always quiet and serious?"

Jacen forced a laugh. "Yeah, I guess you're right."

Tenel Ka continued, "We have discussed this, Jacen. Please do not assume that I need cheering up, that I am helpless, or that I have somehow turned into a whimpering weakling. I am still a Jedi trainee, and I believe I will still become a Jedi Knight . . . as soon as I figure out how."

Jacen reached over tentatively to rest his fingers on her arm and slid them down until she caught his hand in her strong grip.

"If there's any way I can help you, let me know," he said.

She gave his hand a brief squeeze. "I will."

The wavespeeder cruised around a set of sharp rock points that thrust up from the water. The Dragon's Teeth, Tenel Ka called them. The jagged pinnacles hunched together, and the surging waters spurted between them with a slamming sound, regularly erupting in a geyser of white foam.

The engines roared as the craft turned to skirt the turbulence near the Dragon's Teeth, then picked up speed again, shooting out toward the open waves. Jaina and Lowie studied the course, each making calculations and trying to guess how far the craft might take them before they circled back.

"It's about time for lunch," Jacen said, rummaging through the food baskets and handing out meal packets.

When Lowie roared in agreement, Em Teedee said, "Well, of course, Master Lowbacca—aren't you *always* hungry?" The young Wookiee chuffed with laughter, but did not disagree.

The wind from their passage whipped spray in their faces, and the salty-fresh air made Jacen ravenous. He and his friends ate the self-warming meal packs and filled their cups from a thermal beverage container.

Jaina stared through the wavespeeder's transparisteel windscreen while she munched. She glanced at the course again. "I wonder how far this is going to take us."

Up ahead Jacen noted that the water seemed to have a different color and consistency . . . to be more greenish and rough-looking.

Lowie sniffed, sniffed more deeply, then growled a query. Em Teedee answered, "I couldn't tell you, Master Lowbacca—my scent analyzers can't seem to match this with the appropriate data to provide a clear answer. Salt, of course, iodine . . . and some sort of decomposing biological matter, perhaps?"

Jacen caught it too: a sick, sour stench that clogged the air and weighed it down. "Smells like dead fish."

Tenel Ka narrowed her eyes in concentration. "And rotting seaweed. Something very old is there. Something . . . not healthy."

Jaina scanned their course again. "Well, the wavespeeder's taking us right toward it."

Before anyone else could speak, they cruised into the strange, gelatinous area. The water was covered with leafy, floating seaweed as dense as jungle undergrowth. Thick, rubbery tentacles with long wet thorns glistened in the water. Huge, scarlet flowers as big as Jacen's head opened up in the thickest portions of the morass.

Jacen leaned over the edge of the wavespeeder to get a better look. The center of each fleshy-lipped flower held a cluster of moist blue fruits that made the entire blossom look like a wide-open eye. This impression was heightened when the wavespeeder's passing triggered some sort of reflex and the petals of the floating plants blinked closed like eyelids squeezing shut.

"Weird," his sister said next to him.

"Interesting," he replied.

Ahead, the tangled mass of spiny seaweed extended as far as they could see. The wavespeeder continued automatically across the undulating surface of the water, and the foul smell grew stronger. The thick stems and fronds of weed twitched, as if moving by themselves, although Jacen decided it must be caused by swirling currents in the water underneath.

Some of the large eye-flowers rose on their stalks and turned in their direction, as if studying them. Jacen shivered and glanced at Jaina. "Uh, then again . . . maybe 'weird' *is* a better word for it," he agreed.

Lowie looked around, moaning uneasily. Jaina met the Wookiee's gaze and bit her lower lip. "Yeah, I've got a bad feeling about where this boat is taking us. I don't know if I want to go any deeper into this seaweed desert."

"But we're stuck with the autopilot, aren't we?" Jacen said. "If you shut it off, how'll we get back?"

The young Wookiee barked an answer at the same time as Jaina replied, "Been keeping an eye on the course. Lowie and I could probably find our way back home. Ought to be pretty easy."

Tenel Ka stood up, scanning the seaweed, as if trying to remember something. "Jaina is right," she said. "We should return now. To remain here would be unwise."

Jaina and Lowie took over the controls, throttling back while they disengaged the autopilot. As they eased the craft around to head back out of the seaweed, the engine sputtered to a stop.

Since he loved to investigate strange plants and animals, Jacen took the opportunity to lean over the side of the speeder again. He reached down to touch the rubbery, interesting-looking seaweed.

Suddenly, every red eye-flower swiveled to stare at him.

"Whoa!" Jacen said. He waved his hand experimentally, and the flowers turned, attracted by the motion.

Intrigued, he reached for the closest blossom—

and a slick tentacle of seaweed whipped up to wrap around his wrist, capturing him in its barbed embrace.

"Hey!" he shouted. Thorns stung his arm. The seaweed began to pull. "Help!"

He grabbed the railing of the wavespeeder with his free hand to keep from being yanked into the mass of ravenous seaweed. The tentacles thrashed wildly now . . . *hungrily*. Other fronds reached up to slap the side of the boat, twining themselves about the rail.

Lowbacca leaped from the nearby pilot station and grabbed his friend's legs just as the tentacle, redoubling its efforts, gave a sharp jerk and pulled Jacen over the railing. He dangled over the water, struggling to free his arm from the seaweed.

Tenel Ka suddenly appeared beside them. Wrapping her legs around the deck rail, one of her throwing knives gripped tightly in her hand, she bent to slash at the tentacle that grasped Jacen's arm. The seaweed cut free with a snap, and in the recoil Lowbacca managed to yank Jacen back onto the deck.

"Blaster bolts!" Jacen cried, wiping blood from the oozing wounds on his hand. "That was close."

But it was just the beginning. With dread, he looked at the water all around them. The seaweed roiled angrily in every direction, as far as the eye could see. Large fronds thrashed into the air, grabbing the deck rails, as if intending to heave the wavespeeder down. The monster had tasted Jacen's blood, and now it had decided that Jedi Knights were exactly what it wanted for lunch.

Another writhing tentacle rose above the boat's side, searching for a target to skewer with its thorns. Tenel Ka leaped in front of the deadly frond, wielding her throwing dagger. She stabbed into the thick stem of seaweed, and a syrupy green ooze gushed out.

The seaweed recoiled, then lashed back, slapping Tenel Ka across the side of the head. A trickle of blood traced a scarlet line down her cheek. Rather than cry out in pain, Tenel Ka chose to respond with her knife, slashing through the coiled weed—and another fat tentacle thumped to the deck.

Jacen shook his injured arm to restore the feeling then grasped the lightsaber clipped at his side. He had not used it in some time, but there was no room for hesitation now—not if he ever intended to be a Jedi Knight . . . not if any of them wanted to get out of this mess alive. He flicked on the emerald-green blade. "I'm not letting some *weed* get the best of me!" he said.

The humming weapon sliced off one of the large tentacles twined around the rail. "Take that," Jacen said. Gray fumes burned his eyes as the chunk of severed seaweed fell away.

Out in the water the tentacles thrashed. Now they

seemed to be in pain. The scarlet eye-flowers blinked and gyrated furiously. The smell of seared vegetables and saltwater filled the air.

"I'm getting us out of here," Jaina called from the controls, restarting the engines. But grasping tentacles held them in place, and the wavespeeder could not break loose.

Roaring, Lowbacca ignited his own blazing lightsaber and held ît with both hands, a glowing bludgeon of molten-bronze light.

Larger stems rose now from the deeper water, each with a pair of serrated shells on the end, like vicious pincers ready to tear apart prey. The tentacles writhed and clacked their sharp edges together, looking for something to bite into.

Jaina pushed hard on the controls. The wavespeeder's engines whined as it strained against the grasping tentacles.

Lowie raced to the rail. Bellowing a warning, he swept down with his lightsaber blade again and again, slicing through the seaweed that still held their craft.

"Oh, do be careful, Master Lowbacca—here comes another one!"

Grunting a reply, Lowie slashed at the tentacle, and the little translating droid said, "Excellently done, Master Lowbacca! And it's *quite* a comfort to hear you would rather I didn't wind up as an appetizer for a mass of salivating seaweed."

Tenel Ka turned to fend off an attack from one of the sharp-shelled tentacles. She slashed with her knife, but one of the clamshell pincers clenched the point of her dagger with a loud click. The razor-edged shells clacked again, pushing to reach closer to her face.

Then Jacen was there, chopping the tentacle away with his brilliant green energy blade. He flashed Tenel Ka a roguish grin. "Just wanted to keep the score even!"

"My thanks, Jacen," she said.

Lowie hacked with his blade, severing the last of the seaweed tentacles holding the boat. The wave-speeder broke loose and lurched away while thorny fronds writhed and lashed out, struggling to recapture their prize.

As quickly as she could, Jaina pushed the wave-speeder to its highest velocity, roaring over the twisted weed. The malevolent eye-flowers stared at them. Other thrashing tentacles rose up, but the seaweed seemed unable to respond fast enough.

Jacen gripped his emerald-bladed lightsaber, ready. This thing was more than a plant. It was . . . something sentient, something that could *respond*. He used the Force, hoping to calm it, make it leave them alone. "I can't find its brain," he said. "It seems to be all reflexes. All I can sense is that it's hungry, *hungry*."

"Yeah, well it's going to stay hungry a while longer," Jaina said.

"Yes, indeed! I agree wholeheartedly," Em Teedee answered.

Moments later they were out into open water again. Jaina and Lowie plotted their new course, made the appropriate calculations, and manually set the wavespeeder's direction to take them back to the Reef Fortress.

Glancing over at Tenel Ka to make sure she wasn't hurt, Jacen was surprised to see her wearing a calm and satisfied expression as she slid her throwing dagger back into its sheath at her waist. She seemed more alive and confident now than he had seen her at any time since their fateful light-saber duel on Yavin 4.

"We are fine warriors," Tenel Ka said. "There is nothing like a physical challenge to make the day more relaxing."

Lowbacca gave a low grunt. Em Teedee bleeped, but refrained from articulating a comment. Jaina looked at Tenel Ka in surprise, but Jacen laughed. "Yeah, we *are* quite a team, aren't we? Real young Jedi Knights."

Tenel Ka helped Jacen bind up the minor wounds on his arm, and he applied some salve from the wavespeeder's emergency medkit to the stinging cut on her cheek. "I do not believe Ambassador Yfra had this in mind when she sent us out for a day of recreation," she said, "but I found it enjoyable nevertheless."

Lowbacca growled and pointed toward the navigation console. "Oh, dear! Master Lowbacca suggests that it might, perhaps, be premature to feel safe and comfortable quite yet," Em Teedee translated. "You see, he hypothesizes that this wavespeeder was purposely sabotaged."

"What do you mean?" Jacen asked. "Those numbers don't mean anything to me."

"I think he means *this*." Jaina nodded down at the console, indicating the preprogrammed course coordinates. "The autopilot was set to take us into the middle of that killer seaweed—with no return course!"

17

THE GURGLING, SHUSHING sound of gentle waves lapping against stone docks and anchored boats filled the cave grotto. With each breath, Tenel Ka drew comfort from the salty smells and the cool, solid rock around her. Sitting with bare, crossed legs, using a Jedi calming technique to help herself think clearly, she let her gaze drift across each of her friends.

Jaina, head under the control panel and feet high in the air, checked the wiring of the wavespeeder's directional controls. Lowbacca tinkered with the navigational computer from above, handing Jaina tools as she asked for them. Tenel Ka felt a pang of loss as she watched her two friends working with such confidence and agility, completely unconscious of how easy it was for them to use either one hand or the other.

Jacen lay stomach down on a ledge beside Tenel Ka, his right hand reaching deep into the water while the fingers of his left teased the surface, trying to lure a glowing amphibious creature close enough to grasp it.

"Hand me that hydrospanner, would you, Lowie?" Jaina said in a muffled voice. "I need to take this access plate off." Without looking up from his work, the Wookiee plucked the tool from the case behind him with one nimble-fingered hand and passed it to Jaina.

It is so simple with two arms, Tenel Ka thought. As quickly as the jealousy rose within her, she squelched it, chiding herself for being irrational. Even if she still had both hands, she might not have been able to do the things Lowbacca could do with his long, limber arms. He used everything he had, body and mind, to the best of his ability. Just as Jacen and Jaina did.

Just as Tenel Ka always had.

Was she still that same determined person, using her skills and abilities to their fullest, she wondered, or was that person gone now that she had lost her left arm?

She scowled at the thought. If the missing limb was the only thing that bothered her, then surely she could have accepted the biosynthetic replacement her grandmother offered. . . . So perhaps the injury itself was not her primary problem, after all.

Tenel Ka noticed then that Jacen had propped himself up on his elbows and had turned to look at her, his eyes serious. "Hey, you fought really well out there yesterday, against that killer seaweed."

"You mean for a girl with only one arm?" Tenel Ka said bitterly.

"I . . . no, I—" Jacen's cheeks turned crimson and he looked away. His voice was low when he spoke again. "Sorry. All I remembered was you fighting that plant. I didn't even think about your missing arm—it didn't slow you down a bit."

Tenel Ka flinched as if he had slapped her. He was right, she realized: she had not fought like some weak, pitiable invalid. Instinctively, she had battled with everything in her repertoire, drawing on all of her resources. She had truly been *herself*, using every weapon at her disposal.

"Do not be sorry, Jacen," she said. "Your words were meant kindly. It is I who must apologize." She thought again of the battle, musing over what she had accomplished. "I might have fought better, though, if I—"

"—if you had had your other arm?" Jacen finished for her. "Hey, *I* might have fought better if I'd had a blaster cannon, but I didn't. I just did my best."

"No." Tenel Ka looked at him in surprise. "I meant to say, I might have fought better had I used a lightsaber."

With a hesitant smile, Jacen looked up at her again. "Yeah . . . you're pretty good with a light-saber. Of course, you're pretty good at a lot of things."

This was a fact, she thought in wonderment. She was indeed good with a lightsaber. *Still*. And she was also still a good swimmer, fighter, runner. But she had stopped believing in herself, stopped using every portion of her body and mind to their fullest ability. These things were an integral part of the person Tenel Ka had always prided herself in being—and *that* was what she had been missing since the accident.

"Thank you, my friend," she said. "I had begun to forget who I was."

He dazzled her with one of his famous lopsided grins. "Hey, if it was as dangerous to be *me* as it is to be *you*, I might try to forget who I was, too."

"There, that ought to do it." Jaina's voice was loud and clear as she climbed out of the wavespeeder. Lowbacca growled and gesticulated.

"Yep," Jaina agreed. "Sabotage, no doubt about it." With her usual directness, Jaina looked at Tenel Ka and asked, "Any possibility your grandmother could be behind this?"

Jacen gulped. The thought had not occurred to him. "Your grandmother? She wouldn't try—!"

Tenel Ka considered the question seriously. "No," she said at last. "Had that been my grandmother's intention, she would have . . . disposed of me long before you arrived." Lowbacca gave an interrogative growl, and Tenel Ka continued. "Do not misunderstand me. I believe her capable of murder—but I also *sense* that her intention is to keep me from danger, to protect me, whether I become a queen or a Jedi."

Lowbacca growled a reply, and Em Teedee said, "Master Lowbacca points out—and quite rightly, I might add—that with Ta'a Chume traveling back and forth between here and the Fountain Palace, as she did today, she can hardly be counted on to provide protection."

"Well, she did leave some guards on duty," Jaina said.

"And Ambassador Yfra," Jacen added, rolling his eyes. "Oh boy."

Jaina bit her lower lip. "Yfra's the one who suggested we go out in the wavespeeder, you know."

Lowbacca barked a comment. "Not to mention the fact that she claims to have programmed the wavespeeder herself," Em Teedee supplied. "Oh, my!"

Tenel Ka, who had never trusted Ambassador Yfra, made no comment as her friends voiced their suspicions. In the distance she could hear the sound of the large Hapan Water Dragon approaching. "Perhaps it would be safest for the moment to trust no one," she suggested.

Jaina and Lowbacca agreed.

"And maybe we'd better stay as far away from Ambassador Yfra as possible," Jacen added.

Just then, the royal yacht floated into the grotto on a wafer-thin cushion of air. Tenel Ka's grandmother stood at the helm. Ta'a Chume brought the Hapan Water Dragon to a complete stop near one of the stone piers and climbed out onto the dock while her guards secured the craft.

Stepping forward to greet her grandmother, Tenel Ka tried to sense any harmful intentions the matriarch might have. The only emotions she picked up, however, were weariness, frustration, and a sense of grim determination.

"We had one of the bomb conspirators in our grasp today," her grandmother said in a tired voice, "but before I managed to question her, she was poisoned." Ta'a Chume shook her head. "She was under guard the entire time. I don't see how an assassin was able to get to her so quickly."

"You appear to require rest, Grandmother," Tenel Ka said, trying not to seem unduly concerned at the former queen's haggard appearance. "Perhaps you should not conduct this investigation yourself."

Ta'a Chume's eyes narrowed shrewdly. "For decades I ruled the entire Hapes Cluster by myself." The woman sighed and seemed to relent. "But perhaps you are right. I will send Ambassador Yfra back to the mainland to continue the search."

Tenel Ka bit her tongue to keep from voicing her suspicions that Yfra might sabotage the investigation rather than help it. But at least such an assignment would get the possibly murderous ambassador away from the Reef Fortress. Far away.

18

BY NOW ZEKK considered his lightsaber an old friend.

Though he had not taken the time or care to build his own weapon, he practically lived with the scarlet beam. He knew how to make it dance against imaginary enemies. He had fought and defeated every simulated monster the computers could portray in the training room. He had slain mynocks, Abyssins, krayt dragons, wampa ice monsters, piranha beetles, and hordes of angry Tusken Raiders.

In one battle he had even felled a ferocious rancor with his lightsaber. After that difficult victory, Zekk wished he could have watched the reaction of his rival Vilas, who seemed so enamored of the hideous beasts.

Now Zekk strode beside Brakiss as the Master of the Shadow Academy led him down corridors toward the station's central hub. Busy with his training, Zekk had never thought to venture here before. No longer an underconfident and overwhelmed trainee, Zekk walked in his full leather

168

armor with ease, lightsaber at his side, as if he were almost Brakiss's equal.

The Shadow Academy Master seemed quiet and withdrawn, though. The perfectly chiseled features of his handsome face were set in an unreadable mask, his forehead showing just a trace of a frown.

Zekk cleared his throat, finally curious enough to speak. "Master Brakiss, I sense . . . uneasiness in you. You haven't told me about this next exercise. Is there something I should know?"

Brakiss paused and fixed the young man with a calm, piercing gaze. "You are about to face your most difficult trial, Zekk. Everything depends on this. You must demonstrate how talented you truly are."

Zekk lifted his chin and drew a deep breath, flaring his nostrils. His hand moved instinctively to his lightsaber. "I'm ready for anything."

They reached a thick metal door, and Brakiss punched in a code that opened pneumatic locks. The heavy hatch opened slowly, revealing a small air-lock chamber and a second sealed metal door blocking the other side.

Brakiss said, "Trust in your abilities, Zekk. Feel the Force."

Zekk nodded solemnly. "As always, Master Brakiss. I will pass your test. But why is this so important? Why should you be so concerned?"

Brakiss gestured the young man inside the chamber. Zekk entered and stood waiting, but Brakiss remained outside. "Because it will be a fight to the death," he said, then slammed the door, locking Zekk inside.

Within the echoing airlock chamber, Zekk waited. Master Brakiss's words reverberated in his mind. The doors remained sealed, and he forced himself to breathe calmly, though he felt claustrophobic and trapped. Drawing his trusted lightsaber, he gripped it until his knuckles turned white, but he did not yet turn on the blade.

The seconds pounded by, and still the other door didn't open. Fear swelled within him, but he pushed it aside. A Jedi had no place for fear, no reason to fear. The Force was in all things, and the dark side was his ally.

Still, although Zekk had defeated ferocious creatures in the simulation chamber, those opponents had been mere phantoms. He knew that many more dangerous things might happen in a real battle with a real opponent.

He looked at the inner door, wondering if he should hack it open with his lightsaber and force his way free. He needed to see what lurked on the other side. Was this perhaps part of the test? How long should he wait?

Patience, he told himself. He began to count to a hundred—but before he reached ten, the automatic locks on the inner door gave a thump that vibrated through the metal wall. The door swung open by itself.

Zekk felt a disorienting lurch as he stepped out into well-lighted *nothingness.* . . . The floors and ceilings and walls spun about in a blur until he finally realized that he had tumbled into a chamber where the artificial gravity had been turned off— the zero-gravity arena at the hub of the Shadow Academy! He floated free in the open air of the spherical chamber, with no sense of down or up, with nothing to stop his motion.

Zekk's stomach gave a lurch, but he drew a deep breath and concentrated on not throwing up. He focused on the images around him, trying to snatch answers from the briefest glimpses. Grasping the hilt of his lightsaber, he slowed his weightless tumbling and balanced himself. Only then did he notice the seats and standing areas that studded the walls of the chamber, the dozens of noisy onlookers, the balconies pasted on at haphazard angles to accommodate spectators in zero gravity.

Stormtroopers stood in ranks, gripping the balcony rails. The other students at the Shadow Academy sat all around, ready to watch the spectacle. He stiffened, wondering just how difficult this test was going to be. What had Brakiss meant? What was Zekk supposed to do now?

Boulders like miniature asteroids floated in the center of the open arena, along with metal boxes, small cargo containers, and artificial geometrical constructions. Long durasteel pipes drifted free. Zekk could make no sense of the random mix of large and small objects.

Suddenly he understood: they were obstacles.

On the curved wall at the far side of the arena, Zekk saw the clear blister of an observation dome. With his sharp eyesight he spotted figures inside, figures he recognized: the silver-robed figure of Brakiss; the intimidating Nightsister Tamith Kai, with her voluminous ebony hair and her black-spined cape; and the black-armored figure of Qorl the TIE pilot.

Master Brakiss leaned forward and spoke into a voice amplifier. His words boomed through the amphitheater, and all background noise faded.

"You are all here to witness the selection of a leader for our new Dark Jedi trainees—a leader who shall be the first general of our Shadow Academy forces when the Second Imperium makes its grand foray to reclaim the galaxy. Here, before you, we will witness the great battle."

On the other side of the chamber, where the view was partially blocked by drifting obstacles, another airlock opened, and a dark figure emerged. Because of the floating debris, Zekk couldn't see who it was.

Brakiss continued, "This will be a duel to the death between Zekk"—he paused, but none of the students cheered; they knew better, for they would have to follow whoever the victor of this contest might be—"and Vilas!"

Zekk turned, keeping his lightsaber handle in front of him as he faced the thick-browed young man from Dathomir, Tamith Kai's most powerful trainee. Vilas held his ignited lightsaber ready for the duel.

Vilas pushed off from the far wall and flew toward the obstacles at the center. Zekk switched on his weapon and did the same, moving to meet his opponent in the open space. Zekk's heart pounded, and he realized that despite his anxiety, this was a battle he had longed for. How many times since he'd come to the Shadow Academy had Vilas been his rival? After today there would be no question as to who the greater student was.

Vilas shouted in his mocking, oily voice, "If you surrender now, young trash collector, I may only cripple you." He laughed. Zekk felt himself flush. Norys or one of the other Lost Ones must have told Vilas their derogatory nickname for him. *Trash collector.*

Zekk reached the floating debris and found a

pitted oblong stone, an iron-hard meteorite. He grasped it. "If you think victory is going to be *that* easy, Vilas, I'll defeat you before you can blink!"

Zekk hurled the stone with all his strength. In zero gravity the meteorite shot toward the other Dark Jedi—but the equal and opposite reaction after he threw the stone surprised Zekk, and he found himself tumbling backward from the momentum. He slammed headfirst into one of the floating metal cargo containers. A flash of bright pain burst inside his skull. His ears rang. He cleared his vision just in time to see Vilas easily nudge himself out of the path of the flying rock.

Vilas laughed. "Is that the best you can do, trash collector?"

Zekk realized he had been foolish. He concentrated, using the abilities he had recently acquired. Since Vilas was no longer looking at the stone, Zekk used the Force to yank it back toward his enemy. The rock didn't have enough distance to build up much speed, but it struck a sharp blow to Vilas's shoulder. The other young man cried out, rebounding from the impact.

Zekk found himself floating out of control, unable to move where he wanted. He couldn't swim through the air, and he felt entirely disoriented. The walls spun around him. Finally, his feet pressed against the side of a drifting cargo container, and he

propelled himself toward Vilas again. His lightsaber
drew a fiery streak through the air as he plunged
forward.

Vilas was ready for him, though, his glowing
energy blade held up as he spun forward. The two
opponents approached like colliding cannon balls.

Zekk swung, and Vilas met his lightsaber with his
own. The blades clashed and sparked. Bolts of
electricity splashed off in random directions. Then
Zekk shot past while Vilas scrambled in the empty
air, trying to pursue.

Zekk tried to locate one of the floating obstacles
for something else to bounce off of—but suddenly
Jedi instinct warned him to twist out of the way. In
that instant, Vilas came flying by, his lightsaber
slashing and humming through the air. Zekk contorted as if leaping backward over a low fence—but
not quite fast enough. His enemy's fiery weapon
skimmed too close, nicking Zekk's prized leather
armor and leaving a smoking gash.

When Vilas turned with a hoot of victory, Zekk
felt anger boil up from the depths of his mind,
allowing him to draw more strongly on the dark
side of the Force. Reaching out into the floating
debris, he grabbed a pyramidal greenhouse module
and smashed the massive object into Vilas with
enough force to shatter its transparisteel panes.

As Vilas reeled, he chopped with his lightsaber to

cleave the greenhouse module in half. The two smoldering portions tumbled in opposite directions.

His face contorted with rage, Vilas kicked off of one of the floating segments and hurtled toward Zekk, who waited with his lightsaber held low. Vilas made ready to swipe his blade across the space where Zekk was. Zekk knew that if their blades clashed again, the momentum would send them both tumbling out of control. Just as Vilas drew back his lightsaber for a mighty blow, Zekk used the Force to give himself a sharp shove— *away.*

Vilas swept out with full force—and the energy blade buzzed through empty air. Because nothing had stopped the stroke of his sword, Vilas spun about like a slow tornado, tumbling and disoriented.

Zekk saw his opportunity to buy time. He shot up behind one of the larger meteoroids hanging in the center of the weightless arena and plastered himself to the rock surface, pressing his back against the rough stone.

He could hide here for a moment, and then come back fighting.

Inside the arena's observation blister, Qorl remained standing while Brakiss and Tamith Kai both sat in padded chairs, watching their respective champions and hoping for a personal victory. Qorl tried to hide his uneasiness, but could not divert his attention from the two talented young opponents fighting viciously out in the zero-gravity chamber.

Tamith Kai's eyes blazed with violet fire as she fixed upon the battle. She spoke out of the corner of her wine-dark mouth, mocking Brakiss. "Your boy has no chance," she said. "Vilas is much more ruthless. I have trained him. Vonnda Ra has trained him. Even Garowyn has trained him. That young man is the culmination of our efforts on Dathomir. Why bother with this wasteful contest? Just give Vilas command of the new Dark Jedi."

Brakiss sat, exuding outward calm, though Qorl could tell from the subtle reflexive expressions on his face each time the battle reached a new peak that this duel had filled the Shadow Academy Master with tension.

"Ah, Tamith Kai," he said, "you forget that *I* trained young Zekk. That counts for more than all the schooling of all your Nightsisters put together."

Tamaith Kai tore her gaze away from the contest and glared at him. She gave a derisive snort.

"I think," Qorl said, "that Tamith Kai has a point. This type of contest is an utter waste—no matter what the outcome, we still lose our second-best trainee, someone far superior to any of the others we keep."

"This is a different kind of contest," Brakiss said,

as if explaining to one of his students. "Those other trainees know their places and will follow orders without second thoughts. These two, though . . . each thinks he is best. But only one can command. Only one can be the greatest warrior. If we allowed the loser to live, he would always resent the rule of the other—perhaps even try to undermine his authority. No, it is better that we see who is the stronger."

Tamith Kai agreed. "Yes. It is good for the other Jedi trainees to see one of their number die. Only then will they understand the depth of our convictions . . . and realize that the Second Imperium may demand the supreme sacrifice of them, as well." Brakiss nodded.

Qorl made no answer. He did not wish to argue with his two superiors. Obviously, both Brakiss and Tamith Kai believed in the process; who was he to question it? And even if one of the two contestants out there were to forfeit the battle in hopes of saving his life, it would be a terrible blow to morale. *Surrender is betrayal,* after all. Qorl leaned forward to watch the struggle.

But he still thought it a wasteful exercise.

Zekk tried to catch his breath. He couldn't hide for long, of course—not in front of so many cheering spectators, who were growing more and more enthralled as the battle grew more vicious. His hands were slippery with sweat, and he knew he couldn't afford to lose his weapon at the wrong moment during this battle. He would have to be alert and aggressive. Just to be certain, he locked his lightsaber in the ON position and cast about in his mind for a plan that might let him take out Vilas once and for all.

Then, behind him through the rock, he heard a crackling sound and instinctively threw himself away just as Vilas's blazing blade sliced completely through the meteoroid, leaving each chunk of tumbling rock with a flat edge that was so smooth it looked like a molten mirror.

If he hadn't moved at the last instant, the lightsaber would have bisected Zekk just as it had the meteoroid!

He turned in the air to see Vilas hurtling toward him, slashing again. Zekk raised his blade to meet the other lightsaber, and their edges crossed in a shower of sparks. They pushed against each other, but found nothing for traction in weightlessness. They drifted aimlessly, blades locked, jaws clenched, glaring defiantly into each other's eyes.

When Vilas's eyes were drawn for a moment to a point just behind Zekk's shoulder, Zekk barely had time to wonder what his opponent was doing before a drifting metal rod crashed into the small of his back, sending an avalanche of pain along his spine. He gasped, then released his held breath in a rush. His lightsaber, still blazing, tumbled out of his hand.

The crowd roared as Zekk flailed in the air, trying to move away from his opponent. With an evil grin, Vilas charged toward him. Zekk could not reach his lightsaber in time: it spun like a fiery glowrod toward one of the balconies, where spectators scrambled to get out of the way.

With no weapon at hand, Zekk reached beside him to grasp the still-drifting metal rod. He grabbed the pole and swung it through the air with such speed that it made a sighing sound. But, in zero gravity, he was on the other end of the pivot point, and he began to spin around like a baton.

Vilas slashed at the oncoming metal pipe, slicing off half a meter of it. Zekk continued to spin, and Vilas swung again. The blow went wide. Zekk jabbed with the superheated end of the severed pipe, and the hot tip burned through Vilas's armor, searing his ribs.

Vilas yowled in pain and grabbed the pipe himself, flinging it sideways and using the momentum to toss Zekk free. Zekk sailed across space, rebounded off one of the floating meteoroids, and reached out with his mind to call his lightsaber back to him. The weapon stopped its spiraling plunge toward the wall, reversed itself, and zipped into his grasp.

When Zekk turned and looked for Vilas again, though, he found that his opponent had vanished. The brooding young man from Dathomir was hiding, just as Zekk had. Zekk narrowed his eyes and opened his mind to the Force, listening, trying to sense Vilas among the obstacles.

The noise of the crowd gave him no hints . . . but somehow he was able to hear a faint *tink-tink-tink,* coming from behind two joined cargo containers. Zekk struck out for that point. He didn't know what Vilas was doing, but he wouldn't give the other young man time to complete his plan.

Zekk used the Force to direct himself toward the noise, but when he grabbed the edge of the cargo container and pulled himself around it, his lightsaber at the ready, he found only a small chunk of rock invisibly tapping itself against the metal wall. Vilas had managed to distract him, creating a diversion with the Force, while he hid elsewhere and prepared to strike—

With a sudden powerful premonition, Zekk whirled. Vilas *had* to be coming for him. Using his instinct, his sense with the Force, Zekk acted without thinking.

Before he could see, before he could consider what he was about to do, he pulled back to strike with his lightsaber, putting everything he had behind one powerful stroke.

In that instant, through the blaze of light smearing across his eyes, he saw Vilas launch himself out of the cargo container, wearing a predatory grin. He had hidden in ambush, hoping to kill the unsuspecting Zekk.

But Zekk had outsmarted him.

Zekk's slashing blade encountered resistance as Vilas flew across his path. Then, with a flash of smoke and a terrible stench, the bright energy blade cleaved through flesh and bone, cauterizing as it went. Vilas made a choking, gurgling sound and continued his tumbling flight through the air—but now his body moved in two separate, smoking pieces.

Vilas's death rattle was swallowed up in the triumphant roar of the crowd.

Zekk stared down at his pulsating scarlet lightsaber, too horrified at what he had done even to look at the body of Vilas. The spectators still cheered. This had been no simulation, he realized. *This was real.*

Zekk knew he had taken one giant step farther down the road to the dark side. He raised his head, speechless, as the voice of Brakiss echoed through the zero-gravity chamber, drowning out the praise of the onlookers.

"Excellent, Zekk! I knew you could do it."

Tamith Kai's somewhat petulant voice came next. "My congratulations, young Lord Zekk."

Then, to his absolute amazement, overwhelming

even his shock at the violence he had committed, the air in the center of the arena shimmered until an ominous image engulfed the drifting obstacles. The huge hooded head of the Emperor himself offered its grim congratulations directly to Zekk.

"You have won this battle, Zekk," the Emperor said in a voice so filled with cold power it could freeze blood. Zekk drew in a quick gasp. All of the other trainees watched, absorbing their Great Leader's words.

"You are my Darkest Knight, Zekk. I have chosen you to personally lead my Jedi into battle against Skywalker's Jedi academy."

19

THE MUFFLED THUMP of an explosion in the middle of the night was already fading by the time Tenel Ka reacted and sat up, suddenly wide awake.

She strained her ears, but heard nothing more. She had slept fitfully a few times since coming to the thick-walled Reef Fortress—but she had never woken up without cause. Had she really heard the sound of a blast? She couldn't be sure. Perhaps it had merely been a part of her uneasy dream. . . .

Around her, the room was dark and shadowy, lit only by the metallic silver glow of moonlight spilling in from the window. The deep darkness was quiet. Too quiet. With a fluid motion Tenel Ka slid off her bed, stood, paused to listen, then crept forward to the fortress window.

Her skin prickled, but not from cold. She recognized the reaction of her Jedi senses transmitting messages of danger—an indefinable uneasiness that was rapidly growing closer to full-fledged alarm. Something was definitely not right.

Tenel Ka looked out the stone-framed window

down to the glossy midnight ocean that stretched into inky blackness. The breakers, capped with moonlight, crashed against the dark reefs. She heard the rushing, hissing ocean—and realized that the sound should not have been so clear.

Where was the background hum of the night perimeter shields?

Leaning forward, Tenel Ka narrowed her eyes to study the air. A telltale shimmer should have been visible to demonstrate that a protective field surrounded the fortress—but she saw nothing. Then her attention turned to a glimmer of light and a smudge of smoke rising into the air near the generator station.

The shield generator had been destroyed! That meant Reef Fortress now stood unprotected.

Tenel Ka drew back, intending to whirl around and sound the alarm—when a faint motion far below caught her eye. Her heart pounding, all Jedi senses alert, she glanced down to where the steep stone walls blended into the uneven lumps of the reef. A strange camouflaged ship, long and angular, floated just above the waves on repulsorfields.

"Ah. Aha," she said. "Assault craft of some sort." Then she sucked in a sharp breath as she saw figures moving—more than a dozen.

Black, many-legged creatures like large insects swarmed up the base of the fortress—*and scaled the sheer walls effortlessly*. Tenel Ka instantly recognized the tactics, the black body armor, the skittering, segmented movements. Her stomach tied itself into an icy knot, and adrenaline shot through her veins. The Bartokks, deadly humanoid insects, were legendary for their relentless and resourceful assassin squads.

Tenel Ka raced over to the comm unit mounted on a stone wall near her door and slapped the alarm button to sound a general call to arms—but nothing happened. She pushed the alarm firmly once again with her hand, and found that the entire warning system was dead.

"Lights," she called, but her room remained dark. All power, including backup generators, had been cut off to Reef Fortress.

They were in deep trouble.

Bending over and using the stump of her arm to hold the buckle in place, she took a moment to fasten her utility belt over the supple reptilian armor in which she slept. Tenel Ka pulled her hair back with a thong, letting the long red-gold braids drape like a crown around her head. It was time for action. She would have to rouse everyone.

Tenel Ka rushed down the corridor and pounded on the door to Jacen's room. Lowbacca bellowed from his own chamber and flung the door open. Jaina hurried out of the gadget room.

"What's going on?" Jacen asked, dragging unsteady fingers through his sleep-tousled hair.

"Something . . . dangerous," Jaina said, already sensing the situation. "A serious threat."

Lowbacca roared, his wildly disheveled fur standing out in every direction as he attempted to strap on the glossy white belt made of syren-plant fiber. "Emergency?" Em Teedee said. "Perhaps we are all simply overreacting."

"No. We are not," Tenel Ka answered. "The power to the fortress has been cut off, and our defensive force field no longer functions. The generating station has been destroyed. We are currently under attack by a Bartokk assassin squad."

Jacen shuddered. "Hey, I've heard of them. Insects, right? And they all work together as a hive, to assassinate their assigned target."

Tenel Ka nodded. "They are fearsome mercenaries, fighting as one organism. Once given a target, they continue to fight until the very last member of their hive has been killed—or until their victim lies dead."

"I'm sure that's terribly efficient," Em Teedee observed, "but they certainly don't sound very friendly."

Jaina frowned, looking determined. "Well then, what are we waiting for?" She retrieved her lightsaber from her quarters while Jacen ran back into the aquarium room to fetch his weapon, too.

Lowbacca, his lightsaber already at his waist, roared in challenge. "Now, Master Lowbacca, getting delusions of grandeur can be hazardous to your health," Em Teedee said. Lowie just snarled, the black streak across the top of his head bristling with anger.

Tenel Ka stepped into the Wookiee's room, marched to the far wall, and yanked free the jagged ceremonial spear mounted there as ornamentation. Holding the spear one-handed, she said, "We must fight them."

Suddenly they heard a crash and a shout, then brief weapons fire from the far end of the corridor that led to the isolated tower containing the matriarch's quarters.

"My grandmother!" Tenel Ka said. "She must be their primary target."

Still holding the spear, she raced down the cold flagstones of the dim hall. All glowpanels had gone out, and only the moonlight streaming through the corridor windows lit her way—but Tenel Ka had known these twists and turns since childhood.

Growling, Lowbacca sprinted after her while the twins ran at top speed to keep up. Jacen and Jaina ignited their lightsabers, and the brilliant energy glow splashed ahead, shedding enough light for them to see. Tenel Ka heard more shouts, a loud scuffle, and her grandmother's voice calling for help.

"We must hurry," Tenel Ka said, putting on an extra burst of speed. Someone had to have contracted the assassin squad to remove the former queen, she reasoned. Was it Ambassador Yfra? Once Ta'a Chume was dead—and with Tenel Ka's parents gone—the ambassador probably would not consider a one-armed girl in lizard hide much of a threat to her power. She could easily take over the rulership of the Hapes Cluster.

While the idea enraged her, Tenel Ka could not afford to think about it at the moment.

Just ahead, a couple of black, clattering insects emerged from side corridors. The Bartokks, as tall as Tenel Ka, stood on two powerful legs and had a central pair of arms at their waists for grasping and manipulating objects, while their upper set of arms ended in long, hooked claws like scythes used to harvest grain. The serrated edges of the scythe claws swept from side to side, with razor edges that could clip an enemy to pieces.

The Bartokks chittered upon seeing these new and unexpected opponents, but Tenel Ka raced ahead with full momentum. Using all the muscles in her single arm, she jabbed with her spear, plunging it through the body core of the left assassin. Its upper four arms flailed in reflex, trying to bat the weapon out of Tenel Ka's grip—but she twisted the long blade, ripping it sideways. The insect's hard exoskeleton cracked and split open, spilling thick greenish-blue goop onto the stone floor. She yanked the spear free as the Bartokk clattered to the flagstones, its legs still flailing.

Beside her, Lowbacca met the second assassin with a sideways sweep of his lightsaber that sliced the Bartokk into smoking halves that fell twitching to the floor.

The twins rushed up. "Good one," Jacen said, panting. "That's two down."

Tenel Ka spoke over her shoulder as she continued running. "We cannot be certain those two are dead," she said. "And do not forget, the Bartokks have a hive mind. Now all of the assassins—there are usually fifteen in the hive—know we're coming to help my grandmother."

As they skidded around the corner near the armored door to the matriarch's chambers, five more of the insects moved to block their way. Ta'a Chume's two personal guards fought fiercely at the threshold to her chambers, but the remaining Bartokks had nearly succeeded in breaking in.

As the young Jedi Knights ran forward, Bartokk assassins captured both loyal guards outside the matriarch's door and dragged them away. The guards struggled, cried out, then ceased all movement.

Although this capture was intended to free the opening for a fresh assault on the matriarch's chambers, it also created a diversion for Tenel Ka and her friends to plow forward. With their lightsabers ignited, Jacen and Jaina slashed in, chopping the two frontmost Bartokks into quivering bug pieces. Lowbacca barreled into a third assassin, knocking it against the stone wall with such force that its black carapace split open.

"Inside," Tenel Ka shouted. She could hear the matriarch calling for more guards, but there were none. Instead, four young Jedi Knights charged into her chamber.

"Lowie, help me get this closed," Jaina cried. The lanky Wookiee shoved his shoulder against the armored door as he and Jaina swung it shut against the powerful press of Bartokk arms and snapping claws. Startled, most of the insects jerked back, but then began to push and claw at the entrance again almost immediately. In that instant of surprise, however, the door groaned shut.

"Lock it," Jaina gasped, and Tenel Ka snapped a bolt into place.

Outside, Bartokk assassins pounded, scraping with their razor-edged claws against the doorjamb. The metal door rattled in its frame, and Tenel Ka knew their defenses couldn't last long against the onslaught.

But that was the least of her worries at the moment.

Three Bartokk assassins had been trapped *inside* the chamber with them, and now the ruthless black-shelled insects moved forward, focusing on their main target.

The old matriarch had barricaded herself in a

corner and was doing her best to knock the creatures away with a broken piece of furniture. The young Jedi Knights rushed to defend the former queen, but one of the assassins lashed out with its razor claws at them.

Tenel Ka charged forward as the insect killer moved to meet her. She plunged her ornamental spear into it until the tip of her weapon bored all the way through the glossy shell and wedged into a crack between the wall blocks. She left the Bartokk pinned to the wall like a bug in a child's collection. Even so, the creature still writhed and snapped, thrashing to get at them.

Jacen ran forward and with a hissing sweep of his lightsaber, sliced off the multi-eyed head of another assassin as it leapt toward the matriarch.

With a roar, Lowbacca left his post at the rattling door and grasped the remaining Bartokk, lifting it bodily off the floor. Its many sharp arms thrashed as Lowie pushed forward to the high open window and heaved the creature over the ledge. The assassin tumbled nearly thirty meters to splatter on the jagged reef far below.

"Hey!" Jacen said, as the Bartokk he had beheaded, instead of collapsing into twitching death, continued to fight its way toward the alarmed matriarch. "Aren't you supposed to die?"

He slashed again with the lightsaber, this time cutting the legs out from under the headless Bartokk. The insect torso crashed to the floor, but with its remaining limbs it still hauled itself toward Tenel Ka's grandmother. The severed head lay on the flagstones near the wall, staring at its target through faceted eyes, somehow continuing to direct the body.

"These hive-mind assassins," Tenel Ka explained, "their brains are distributed through major nerve networks inside their bodies. Simply cutting off a head won't stop them. The pieces will still attempt to continue their mission."

With another blow from his lightsaber, Jacen chopped the remaining torso in half. "This is getting ridiculous," he said.

Lowbacca marched over to where the severed insect head lay near the wall. Then with great pleasure he stomped down, squashing it as one might step on an annoying beetle.

The wiry old matriarch tossed aside the broken piece of furniture she had been using as a weapon. "I thank you for your efforts to save me, my granddaughter," she said, "but it would seem that this plot is rather extensive. Our entire fortress is overrun, and I see no means of escape."

Across the floor the ichor-dripping pieces of the chopped-up assassin continued to squirm toward the former queen, blindly groping, yet still deadly. The skewered Bartokk hanging from the wall thrashed and flailed, trying to break free from Tenel Ka's spear.

Outside, in the corridors, the rest of the assassin hive hammered without pause against the armored plates of the door. From where Tenel Ka stood, she could see the rivets popping out and blocks crumbling to powder at the edges of the sealed door. The metal began to bend inward. . . .

It certainly wouldn't last much longer.

20

JAINA LOOKED AROUND the dim room where they had barricaded themselves, desperate to find some means of escape. With the hammering of assassins outside the door growing louder and louder, she found it hard to think. Pale moonlight streamed through the window from a deceptively calm sky, bleaching all colors in the room to black and white and gray.

"We have to get out of here somehow," Jaina said.

Tenel Ka nodded grimly. "This is a fact."

Jacen turned to the matriarch. "Hey, if you know of any secret passages that lead out of here, now might be the time to tell us."

"There are none," Ta'a Chume said. "This tower room was designed as a protected chamber, with no secret ways for an assassin to gain entrance. Reef Fortress itself was built to be impregnable."

Jaina snorted. "Maybe you'd better fire your architect."

Tenel Ka felt at her utility belt and removed her

grappling hook and the strong fibercord. "I see no better way. We must escape by the same route those creatures used to break into the fortress. Not only must we flee the fortress, we must flee the reef island itself."

"Where can we go, Tenel Ka?" Jacen said. "We're stranded."

"I get it!" Jaina cried, seeing what her friend intended. "We take one of the fast wavespeeders and zoom out across the ocean. It's our best chance."

The stern matriarch went to the window and gazed at the sheer drop. "You mean *climb* down?"

"Yes, Grandmother," Tenel Ka said, setting the grappling hook firmly against the stone of the windowsill. "Unless you'd prefer using your diplomatic skills to negotiate a settlement with the Bartokks."

The matriarch's sharp eyes flashed with determination. "I've never allowed anyone but myself to control my fate—so I suppose falling to my death while escaping would be preferable to waiting around to be killed by giant insects in my own bedchamber. It's agreed, then. We'll try the climb, as you suggest."

Tenel Ka shook her head. "No, we shall *do* the climb. There is no try."

Jaina tugged on the cord. The grappling hook did not budge. "All right, let's get out of here."

Lowbacca blatted a comment and Em Teedee said, "Oh, dear—*must* I?" At the Wookiee's growled response, the little droid heaved an electronic sigh. "Master Lowbacca believes he would be the most sensible choice to go first—and unfortunately I'm forced to admit that he is correct. Firstly, because he is an experienced climber, and secondly because he is strong and will be able to hold the rope steady for the rest of you once he reaches the bottom."

"Can't argue with your logic," Jaina agreed. "Go ahead."

While Em Teedee twittered about the impending danger, Lowie swung himself over the sill and supported his full weight on the glistening fiber-cord. Then, using his long arms, he lowered himself hand-over-hand down the vertical stone wall. Em Teedee's pitiful moans grew more and more faint until finally Lowie touched down on the rocks below, stood away from the wall, and gave the rope a yank.

"Good," Tenel Ka said.

Persistence finally paid off for the Bartokks, who had continued their relentless battering at the armored door. One of the hinges groaned and popped out of the wall. With a loud creak, a corner of the door bent inward. Chittering insect assassins thrust their sharp scythe claws through the gap.

"No more time," Tenel Ka said to the twins. "You two go now. The rope will hold both of you."

"We'd better be careful," Jacen said. The door rattled in its frame and the metal screeched, caving in further.

"Guess we can't afford that luxury," Jaina said in a terse voice. "What are we waiting for?" She slipped over the sill, grabbing the fibercord, and began rappelling down the slick dark stones.

Jacen came after her. The rope was thin, and the descent treacherous, but they used their Jedi skills to keep their balance and make themselves lighter. At the bottom Lowbacca stood with his feet planted far apart on the rocky reef, holding the rope.

"Excellent climbing, Master Jacen, Mistress Jaina," Em Teedee encouraged. "You're almost here—you can make it!"

Even before they reached bottom, Jaina looked up to see Tenel Ka and her grandmother easing over the sill. The matriarch, unable to grasp the slender cord tightly enough in her old hands, steadied herself with an arm around Tenel Ka's waist. The young warrior girl had looped the rope once around her arm to allow herself more friction to control their descent.

With a firm hold on the fibercord, she slowly leaned backward, letting the strand slip through her fingers as her feet pressed against the outer wall of the fortress. The dangerous climb may have been more difficult and awkward with her handicap, but Tenel Ka did not seem the least bit hesitant. Despite her usual reluctance to use the Force, she took advantage of it this time without reservation.

"Come on, Tenel Ka!" Jacen called.

Before the girl and her grandmother had gotten more than halfway down the rope, though, a loud crash sounded from above. Suddenly swarms of multilegged figures surged to the open window, squealing their triumph.

Jaina heard Tenel Ka shout, "Hold on!" as she doubled her speed, sliding down the cord so quickly that Jaina was sure she would get a rope burn on her hand and arm.

The Bartokks grabbed the fibercord and sawed at it with their serrated scythe arms.

Tenel Ka slipped down faster, faster.

Suddenly the strand parted. The insectoid assassins above gave a triumphant chitter.

Lowbacca roared and with lightning-fast reflexes dropped the end of the severed rope, held out his arms, and caught the old matriarch as she plunged. Using the Force to control her own fall, Tenel Ka landed heavily on her feet, but without injury.

"Good one, Tenel Ka," Jacen cried. "We made it!"

"Not quite yet," Jaina said, pointing upward. The remaining black Bartokk assassins started to boil through the upper window, crawling headfirst down the vertical stone block.

"We must hurry," Tenel Ka said, pointing toward the grotto. "To the wavespeeders."

At the far edge of the reef, Jaina saw the sharp-edged assault boat from the Bartokk hive near the smoldering wreck of the shield-generator station. For a moment she contemplated taking that craft instead—but when she noticed the knobby, alien controls designed for simultaneous use by four claws, she couldn't be sure she or Lowie could pilot such a ship. Their best chance would be to grab one of the smaller wavespeeders.

Ducking under the moss-edged rock of the entrance, they ran into the sea cave. A wavespeeder, tied to the dock closest the entrance, bobbed gently on the water of the grotto.

"Everybody in," Jaina said. "Lowie and I can handle this. Let's just hope its top speed is better than what that assassin craft can manage."

"And that Ambassador Yfra hasn't sabotaged it!" Jacen muttered.

Lowbacca bellowed his agreement. Still dazed after her fall, the grim matriarch shook herself and climbed aboard as Jacen and Jaina hopped over the rail, followed by Tenel Ka.

With a roar, the repulsorlift engines raised the wavespeeder up off the calm waters inside the sheltered cave. Before Tenel Ka had managed to seat herself, Jaina pulled the boat away from the dock, whipped it around, and accelerated through the cave entrance, churning the water into froth beneath them. The wavespeeder shot away from the darkened, overrun Reef Fortress.

Lowbacca, sitting in the navigator's chair, turned his shaggy head to gaze back at the tall citadel with his dark-adapted Wookiee eyes. He growled, stretching out a hairy arm. Jaina risked a glance and saw the insectoid murderers swarming down the tower wall toward their assault craft.

"Better get our head start while we can," Jaina said grimly. She pushed hard against the accelerators, although they were already traveling at maximum speed. The small boat sped out to where the sea grew choppier.

Moments later an ear-splitting mechanical roar erupted behind them. Jacen shouted, and Jaina glanced back to see the Bartokk assault craft pull away from the reef, infested with black insect assassins.

The assault craft's engine thundered like a Star Destroyer in pursuit. "They must have come in using stealth silencers on their engines," Jaina said. "They're at full power now, though—no need to keep quiet." She watched the tactical panel in front of her and swallowed a lump in her throat.

Lowie growled. "Master Lowbacca estimates that they will overtake us within minutes," Em Teedee wailed. "What *are* we to do?"

The ocean was lit only by the twin moons high overhead in the midnight sky. Jaina saw froth ahead as the water surged around a rocky obstacle jutting from the sea—the Dragon's Teeth. "We'll go there," she said, "and try to cause some trouble as they dodge around the rocks. We're smaller, more maneuverable."

"I doubt they'll give up because of a navigation hazard," Jacen said.

"No," Jaina replied, "but we can hope they crash."

The pointed rocks thrust out of the water like jagged spires. Waves crashed against their faces, running like saliva drooling from a krayt dragon's mouth, and rippled around the submerged reefs at the base of the Teeth. The Bartokk assault craft screamed after them.

"Watch the waves—and count," Tenel Ka said, pointing as a plume of white water jetted up between the two sharp rocks. Five seconds later another plume spurted up just as high. "Timing could be our advantage."

Jaina nodded. "I see what you mean. Lowie, I'll need your help on the controls." They slowed just enough to let the assault craft approach them as they headed toward the narrow gap between the treacherous rock spires.

"It's going to be close, Jaina," Jacen said.

"Don't I know it," she agreed. "Okay, punch it, Lowie."

The Wookiee hit the accelerators full force just as the Bartokk assault craft nearly rammed them from behind. The insect assassins waved their clacking arms. One fired a deck-mounted cannon, and the blaster bolt struck the waves, creating a geyser of steam just beside their wavespeeder.

"Whoa," Jaina said as Lowie yowled. "Didn't expect that."

Unconsciously ducking her head as they streaked between the black rocks, she canted the wavespeeder to fit through the narrow gap. The hiss of their passage boomed and echoed, and a fine cold spray splashed them all.

The assault craft charged in behind them. Jaina didn't think the assassins could possibly fit through the narrow opening, but the ship slid into the gap with only a few centimeters of play on either side.

The ocean roiled just as the assault craft spat from the narrow cleft between the rocks. A jet of water rocketed through the gap, shooting out a high-powered plume that catapulted the Bartokk assault craft into the air and spun it end-over-end.

Three assassins toppled overboard and vanished into the churning seas before the assault craft righted itself and crashed back onto the water. The Bartokk pilot wrestled with the controls as Jaina streaked onward at top speed, stretching the gap between them.

Before long, though, the assault craft was hot on their tail again.

Sitting in back, Ta'a Chume recovered enough to reach inside her plush robes and withdraw a tiny holdout blaster. "For what it's worth," the matriarch said, "I'll use this—but it's designed for only two shots."

"What good is a blaster that only has two shots?" Jacen asked.

"The first shot is for an attacker," Tenel Ka's grandmother answered. "The second shot . . . well, sometimes it is preferable not to be taken alive."

Jaina gulped and continued to guide the wavespeeder away from the reef. Waves crashed against the front of their craft, but she couldn't gain any more height from their repulsorlifts. Fortunately, the Bartokk assault craft had sustained some damage in its passage through the Dragon's Teeth, and now the pilot of the impaired vessel had no choice but to hang back.

Pushing the wavespeeder to its redlines, Jaina maintained their lead—but just barely. Another hour went by as they sped over the dark wavetops under the pale light of the moons. The assault craft edged closer and closer.

"Is there any way to get back to civilization, get some help?" Jacen asked.

"Our fortress is extremely isolated—theoretically for our protection—and this wavespeeder travels much too slowly," the old matriarch said. "It would take us many hours to get back. I fear the Bartokks will have taken care of us before then."

"Not if I can help it," Jaina said, gritting her teeth as she diverted them toward a pale patch of water ahead, a wasteland covered with a rough, flattened texture and exuding a spoiled fishy smell. She realized full well where they were going. The coordinates had been familiar, and now she hoped to use her knowledge to their advantage.

Lowbacca, guessing her intention, let out a questioning whine.

"I know what I'm doing, Lowie," Jaina said.

Jacen must have smelled the same thing. He leaned toward his sister in alarm. "You're not actually going into that seaweed field, are you?"

Jaina shrugged. "They'd be crazy to follow us, wouldn't they?"

"The Bartokk assassin hive will follow us to the ends of the planet," Tenel Ka said. "They have no concern for their own danger."

"Good," Jaina said, "then maybe they'll get sloppy."

Suddenly the sound of the engines grew muted as they streaked over the writhing forest of carnivorous seaweed. Just below the hull of their wavespeeder, the weed thrashed in agitation. Clusters of red eye-flowers rose up, keeping a vigilant watch for new prey even in deepest night. The seaweed flickered and snapped, as if it remembered its near miss with the group of young Jedi only days before.

"I sure hope this thing is still hungry," Jacen said. "How about we give it some plant food?"

"As long as it's not us," Jaina responded.

The Bartokk assassins paid no heed to how the sea had changed, intent only on closing the gap between them and their prey.

The matriarch stood at the rear of the wavespeeder, holding her small blaster. "Two shots," she said, pointing her weapon at the approaching boat.

"Target their repulsorpods," Jaina shouted. "That's the only weak spot on a big assault craft like that."

The wavespeeder jostled, but the matriarch took careful aim and fired a high-powered blaster bolt. The streak of energy skimmed the bottom of the pursuing assault craft, leaving the repulsorpod undamaged. The shot reflected off the Bartokks' metal hull and sizzled into the churning seaweed creature.

"No damage," the matriarch said. "One chance left."

"Your shot was not wasted," Tenel Ka said. "Observe the plant."

The seaweed now seemed fully awake and *angry*. Its spined tentacles thrashed in the air and slapped at the craft roaring over its fronds.

The Bartokk assassins approached the wavespeeder, apparently unconcerned that one of their intended victims had just used a blaster. The Bartokk craft fired a return shot with one of its laser cannons, but Jaina, sensing the impending bolt through the Force, rocked the wavespeeder to the left. The blast struck the seaweed again, eliciting a hissing, low-frequency roar from the plant monster.

Ta'a Chume stood again, raised her tiny blaster, and aimed a second and last time.

"May the Force be with you," Tenel Ka murmured.

The matriarch took her final shot. This time the energy bolt struck one of the Bartokk repulsorpods squarely. Though the tiny weapon was not powerful enough to cause great damage, it was enough to throw the pursuing assault craft into a spin.

The stern of the assassins' boat rose up and, as the Bartokk insects scrambled for control, the bow plunged, grazing the ravenous seaweed. Before the pilot could regain stability, a dozen spiked tentacles whipped up to wrap themselves around the rails, snatching at the hull, the repulsorpods, the laser-cannon emplacements. The insect assassins chittered, more in anger than fear, because the hive mind couldn't comprehend its impending death.

Within moments, however, Bartokk assassin legs were flailing as spiked weed tentacles plucked the insects from their stations at the side of the boat and dragged them thrashing beneath the foaming waves. Soon the seaweed had engulfed the entire sharp-edged craft, dragging it under the roiling water.

Pincer-ended tentacles clamped down on hard chitinous shells, and Jaina heard muffled crunching sounds as the seaweed monster snapped exoskeletons apart to reach the tender parts inside. She stared at the water in horrified fascination.

"I think maybe this is our cue to leave," Jacen pointed out, giving his sister a nudge. Lowie roared his agreement.

Bloodred eye-flowers blinked hungrily up at them.

"Okay, what are we waiting for?"

Lowie revved the engines and then accelerated as Jaina guided the wavespeeder back out of the deadly tangle of seaweed.

Ta'a Chume made her way to the front of the wavespeeder. "I can pilot us to safety from here," she said. Jaina gladly relinquished the controls as the former queen headed the craft toward the mainland.

"An excellent shot, Grandmother," Tenel Ka said.

The matriarch nodded and looked with renewed admiration at her granddaughter. "So much for diplomacy."

Some five hours later, the entire bedraggled crew finally hauled themselves into the Fountain Palace.

Ta'a Chume was outraged to find that Ambassador Yfra had already assumed control. Declaring martial law, the ambassador had announced that there would be several hours of mourning over the untimely death of the dear, departed matriarch.

Tenel Ka marched beside her grandmother into the central throne room amidst gasps of horror, delight, and surprise from the guards. The most appalled expression, however, showed on the hardened face of Ambassador Yfra herself.

"Ta'a Chume!" she cried, standing up and trying unsuccessfully to hide the brief storm of anger that clouded her eyes. "You're—you're alive. But how—?"

"Your plot failed, Yfra. Guards, arrest this traitor!"

"On what charge?" Ambassador Yfra said in a reasonable tone, her confidence not yet shaken.

"Plotting to kill the entire royal household. I am only happy that Tenel Ka's parents were absent, for I'm sure they would have been at risk as well."

"Why, Ta'a Chume—I've never shown anything but loyalty to you." Yfra's voice was full of sweetness and offended innocence, though Tenel Ka could sense that she was lying. "How can you make such an accusation?"

"Because you took control. How could you possibly have known we were in danger if you hadn't set up the plot yourself?"

"Well, I—" Yfra blinked. "I simply responded to the distress call sent out from Reef Fortress, of course."

"Ah." The matriarch pointed her long knobby finger and a smile curved her thin wrinkled lips. "Aha! But no distress signal was sent. Your Bartokk assassins blew up our power-generating station. We escaped. This is the first word that has gotten out—but *you* knew." The matriarch nodded confidently. "Yes, you knew."

Before Yfra could sputter another excuse, the guards came forward and took her into custody.

"Oh, she'll be given a fair trial," the matriarch said, "but I think we have more than enough proof—don't you, Tenel Ka?" She raised her eyebrows.

"This is a fact," the young warrior woman replied. "And I believe I have more than enough proof for something else, as well." She stood straight, looking proudly into her grandmother's eyes.

"This adventure has shown me that I am fully recovered from my injuries. I wish to return to Yavin 4."

21

TENEL KA SAT up and looked around with brief disorientation before she remembered where she was. Letting her gray gaze skim across the ancient stone walls, arched doorway, and modest sleeping pallet, she experienced a sense of warmth and safety—and excitement.

It felt right to be back on Yavin 4, in her own student quarters in the Great Temple. She sat back on her pallet and began practicing her new skill—braiding her hair with one hand and her teeth.

Over the past weeks, the wrongness in her life had slowly dissolved, beginning with her parents' safe return to Hapes. Having foiled an attempt on their own lives by Ambassador Yfra's henchwomen, Teneniel Djo and Isolder had hurried back to find their daughter and her grandmother unharmed. They immediately sought out and purged the remaining conspirators from the royal court, while Ambassador Yfra awaited trial.

To Tenel Ka's great surprise, neither of her parents had tried to talk her into wearing a synthetic arm or discontinuing her studies at the Jedi academy. In fact, when she had expressed her desire to continue her training, her mother and father had readily agreed, asking only that she stay to visit with them for a few weeks before returning to Yavin 4.

"I believe you may become a stronger warrior than ever you imagined," Teneniel Djo said. "You have powerful legs, fast reflexes, and you still have your better fighting arm. From what your grandmother tells us, your wits have not been dulled, either."

"And I think you may teach many a future opponent that one cannot judge a warrior's worth by her outward appearance," her father added, hugging her. "Never be ashamed of what you are—or *who* you are."

When Luke Skywalker had returned in the *Shadow Chaser* to take Tenel Ka and the other young Jedi Knights back to Yavin 4, there had been no mistaking her parents' pride. Her mother's final whispered words still echoed through her mind: "May the Force be with you."

Now, after a good night's rest in familiar quarters, Tenel Ka felt ready to take her next step to recovery. She stood and stretched, delighting in the well-controlled response of her muscles.

She spent the next few minutes ransacking her belongings until she had collected the objects she needed. She found her remaining rancor-tooth trophy wrapped in its supple leather covering. She tucked it under the stump of her severed arm—not a completely useless limb after all, she noted with some satisfaction—while she searched for another item. When at last she located the jewel-encrusted tiara from Hapes, which her grandmother had insisted she take, she placed the two articles side by side on a tiny worktable in the corner and studied them.

Both objects were symbols of who she was, of her upbringing. The rancor's tooth came from Dathomir, a planet that was wild, untamed, fierce, and proud. The tiara symbolized her Hapan inheritance: regal bearing, refinement, power, wealth, and political shrewdness.

Tenel Ka had long believed that honoring one part of her heritage implied that she must *dis*honor the other. Just as she had believed that trusting in the Force implied a lack of trust in herself. Wincing at the thought, she was compelled to acknowledge that she had actually gained wisdom from the loss of her arm. She knew now that she had to use every ability she possessed—including her talent with the Force—to become the best possible Jedi.

But what of her heritage? she thought, picking up the rancor's tooth and turning it over in her palm. Hapes and Dathomir. Could she combine the best of both? She was, after all, only one person.

Coming to a decision, she grasped the rancor

tooth tightly, lifted it over her head, and brought it smashing down on the glittering, jewel-studded tiara. The delicate crown broke into pieces.

Tenel Ka hammered again and again until bits of precious metal and gems lay strewn across the tiny table.

Yes, she decided. She was a product of two worlds, and she would learn to blend the best of her mother's *and* her father's. She laid down the rancor's tooth and reached for the other items she had assembled.

Then, selecting the finest jewels from her Hapan tiara, she began to build her new lightsaber.

Brilliant morning sunlight played across the top of the Great Temple and filtered through Tenel Ka's partially braided hair to form a red-gold nimbus around her. Jacen stood about a meter away, facing her, a gentle breeze ruffling his unruly brown curls. His face was filled with apprehension.

"You sure you want to do this?" he asked.

"Yes," she said simply, though she felt an uncertain fluttering in the pit of her stomach.

"Well, I'm not sure *I* can go through with it," he said in a low voice.

"You? But why—"

"Blaster bolts! The last time we did this, I ended up . . ." Jacen's voice trailed off and he looked significantly at what remained of her arm.

"Ah," Tenel Ka said. "Aha."

"So I'm asking you if you're sure," Jacen said, "because I'm not."

Gray eyes searched brandy-brown while Tenel Ka considered this. Her throat was tight with unaccustomed emotion when she finally spoke. "Jacen, my friend, I know of no better way to show that I trust you . . . that I do not blame you for what happened."

Jacen's face was solemn as he nodded his acceptance. "Thank you." He let his eyes fall half shut and took a deep breath.

Tenel Ka did the same, feeling the Force flow into her, through her. Her muscles tautened—not with fear, but with a delicious anticipatory tension. Reaching for the rancor's tooth clipped to her belt, Tenel Ka held it steady in front of her and pressed the power stud.

A blade of sizzling energy sprang from the ivory hilt, glowing a rich turquoise, produced by the rainbow gems she had installed from her tiara. A heartbeat later, Jacen's emerald lightsaber hummed to life.

As if in slow motion, the two friends raised their blades until they hovered at eye level, just centimeters apart. With a crackle of discharged energy, their lightsabers touched once. Then again.

Hesitantly at first, Tenel Ka thrust with her turquoise blade, and Jacen parried with a barely perceptible nod.

The Force flowed between them, around them, and soon they were moving in ancient patterns and rhythms, as in a well-rehearsed exercise routine, an intricate dance. Somehow both of them knew that neither would come to any harm.

Their eyes locked, while the silent music that accompanied their movements built to a crescendo, then began to fade. But their confidence in each other did not wane as their movements slowed.

They stood still at last, lightsabers barely touching, a look of amazement on both of their faces. Jacen opened his mouth as if to speak, but no sound came out.

A moment later, an ear-shattering roar split the air as Lowbacca and Jaina ran across the rooftop to greet them.

Jaina laughed. "I agree with Lowie: it's good to see you holding a lightsaber again, Tenel Ka. For a while I was worried that you thought you were too different from us, that you couldn't be our friend anymore."

"Perhaps for a while I did," Tenel Ka said. "But I have learned that differences can be positive, that they can be blended together to form a stronger whole."

"We *are* pretty different," Jacen pointed out.

Jaina switched on her amethyst energy blade with a snap-hiss. "But we're all going to be Jedi Knights."

Lowbacca ignited his lightsaber as well. Its shaft glowed a molten bronze.

"Stronger together," Tenel Ka said, raising her turquoise lightsaber high over her head.

Lowbacca lifted his lightsaber to touch hers.

"Yes, stronger together," Jacen and Jaina said in unison, crossing their glowing blades with the other two.

The four lightsabers blazed into the morning light.

The bestselling saga continues . . .

STAR WARS®
YOUNG JEDI KNIGHTS

Darkest Knight

The twins and Lowbacca are off to the Wookiee's home planet of Kashyyyk, where Lowie's youngest sister, Sirra-kuk, is about to undergo the terrifying Wookiee rite of passage. The ceremony is difficult and dangerous, and Lowie wants to help her in any way he can.

Meanwhile, the Dark Jedi student Zekk has been given his own rite of passage: to lead a raid on the great Wookiee computer center on Kashyyyk. Finally, he will fulfill his awesome potential. Finally, he will become the Second Imperium's Darkest Knight. But first he must face his old friends Jacen and Jaina, once and for all . . .

Turn the page for a special preview of the next book in the STAR WARS: YOUNG JEDI KNIGHTS series:
Darkest Knight
Now available from Berkley Jam Books!

THE SCREAMING SOUNDS of TIE fighters rippling through the atmosphere of Kashyyyk sent a chill of primal fear down Jacen's spine. He knew the distinctive howl was only the exhaust from the powerful engines, but the Imperial ship designers must have delighted in the hellish noise, which was sure to strike fear into the enemies of the Empire.

In the hustling fabrication facility, alarms rang out from platform loudspeakers in a loud cacophony. Growling, barking announcements hammered through the air. Wookiee workers ran in all directions, activating security systems or evacuating the area.

TIE bombers streaked low over the treetops, dropping proton explosives that set the dense network of branches aflame. Dark gray smoke billowed from burning leaves.

"We must help defend against this threat," Tenel Ka said, looking from side to side for some weapon substantial enough to use against the invading fighters. Her face wore a stony expression of determination.

Sirra and Lowie both howled in rage at seeing the destruction of the tree dwellings. The spindly Tour Droid spun its boxy head around, despite its numerous optical sensors. "Do not panic. Have no fear," it said in a tinny voice. "This must be a drill. No attack has been scheduled for today."

"Schedule or not, we're definitely under attack!" Jacen said.

The Tour Droid continued to issue calming messages, though its thoughts were obviously scrambled. "We have nothing to fear. Kashyyyk has numerous satellite defenses. No enemy ships can approach this facility. We have sophisticated defense mechanisms, including powerful perimeter guns. They should begin firing any moment now."

At Lowie's waist, Em Teedee piped up in a scornful tone. "You silly Tour Droid, switch on your optical sensors! Can't you see this is a crisis situation? Hmmmf!" The miniaturized droid's optical sensors blinked as he muttered a depreciating comment about clumsy public-relations models.

"Didn't the Tour Droid mention perimeter guns?" Tenel Ka said, her slate-gray eyes flashing. "Perhaps we can use them against these enemies."

Sirra roared, gesturing with her long hairy arm to show that she knew the way.

"What a splendid idea," Em Teedee said. "I do hope we aren't blown to bits before we can implement Mistress Tenel Ka's plan. Oh my."

"As my sister would say," Jacen said, "what are we waiting for?"

While the Tour Droid bleated its empty reassurances, Jacen, Tenel Ka, and the two young Wookiees barged past him into the main platforms of the fabrication complex.

Sirra led them down an open-air corridor amid the din of explosions and the crackling shrieks of laser blasts. They reached a network of pulley-driven vines, rapidly moving ropelike lifts that yanked them to a higher level. Sirra grabbed one vine, tucked her foot into a loop, and the rope sprang upward, drawing her toward the higher platforms. Lowie did the same. Jacen followed suit, looking down to watch Tenel Ka, who had no problem whatsoever. She wrapped her arm around the vine and stepped into a loop. Within seconds, they were all whisked to the upper platform at the outer perimeter of the complex.

Because of their quick reaction, the companions reached the defensive guns before most of the Wookiee defenders. Jacen saw unattended ion cannons with spherical power sources and needlelike barrels aimed toward the sky—but his eyes lit upon a pair of old-model quad-laser cannons, exactly like those used in the *Millennium Falcon*'s gun wells.

"There," Jacen said, "we can use those. They're powered up and ready to go." He raced over to the nearest emplacement. Tenel Ka gruffly agreed and stationed herself behind one of the other weapons.

The two Wookiees chattered to each other. Em Teedee called, "Master Jacen! Master Lowbacca and Mistress Sirrakuk have decided to use the computers to determine where the breakdown in the facility's defensive systems occurred. Perhaps they can repair it and prevent further Imperial fighters from getting through. Oh, I do hope they're successful."

"They'll do their best," Jacen said, grabbing the quad-laser's targeting controls. He sank down into the voluminous seat in front of the quad-laser cannon. Reaching out to the widely spread controls designed for a large Wookiee body, he realigned the targeting circle and felt the energy thrum through the firing sticks in his fingers.

Imperial fighters continued to howl overhead, launching strikes against the Wookiee residential districts and targeting the outer platforms of the computer complex, but leaving the central facilities relatively untouched . . . though thrown into complete chaos.

A glance to Jacen's left told him that Tenel Ka had positioned herself and was ready. Gripping the firing stick with her right hand, she familiarized herself with the weapon's control systems. In seconds her eyes began to track the enemy fighters overhead.

Three tall Wookiees charged onto the defensive platform and took up positions at the ion cannons, glancing curiously at the two humans, confused by the unexpected assistance—but they didn't argue. Instead, they fired wild blasts from the ion cannons.

One of the crackling yellow-white shots caught a TIE fighter that soared through the edge of the blast. The Imperial control systems flickered out, and the TIE fighter spun dead in the air, its engine silenced. Unable to regain control, the pilot crashed into the distant forest canopy with a dull, booming explosion.

Jacen used his targeting circles to lock onto a sluggish, fully loaded TIE bomber that arrowed toward the clustered residential structures. The TIE bomber came in, picking up speed, its deadly bomb-bay doors opened.

Jacen grasped the firing controls of the quad-laser cannons and gritted his teeth. "Come on . . . come on," he said. Finally, the target lock blinked as the TIE bomber settled directly in the crosshairs.

He squeezed both firing controls, launching searing blazes of laser energy from all four cannons. The beams targeted on the bomber just before it could drop its proton explosives. Instead of destroying the homes of hundreds of Wookiees, the TIE bomber erupted in midair. The belch of detonations grew louder, echoing as its own proton bombs fed into the eruption, and the brilliant ball of fire and smoke expanded into the sky.

"Got one!" Jacen crowed.

Tenel Ka fired repeatedly until another pair of TIE fighters exploded in the air. "Two more," she said.

By now, more Wookiee defenders had arrived to assume positions at the remaining guns. Jacen fired again and again, rotating his chair to aim at the rapidly moving targets. He blasted another TIE fighter out of the sky.

"Just like our practice runs in the *Millennium Falcon*," he said. "Only this time, hitting the targets is a lot more important than winning a contest with my sister."

"This is a fact," Tenel Ka said.

Another wing of TIE fighters swooped down, and Jacen fired wildly. There were so many Imperial targets, all of them bristling with lethal weaponry. Jacen's quad-laser cannon spat bolts of energy, but they all missed as the fighters spun evasive loops in the air.

"Oh, blaster bolts!" Jacen said.

More Wookiees arrived, leaping off the vine pulley-lifts and rushing to their positions, although now there were more defenders than guns. Lowie and Sirra hurried over to Jacen and Tenel Ka. The young Wookiees spoke loudly, their grunts and growls over-lapping so that Em Teedee had difficulty translating both. Jacen couldn't begin to get the gist of their excited conversation.

"One at a time, please!" the little droid said. "All right, I believe I understand the basics of what you're saying. Master Lowbacca and Mistress Sirrakuk have determined that a single-point defensive failure occurred in the traffic control tower for this facility. Somehow, all of the central command systems have been compromised, as if someone simply took over the station. It appears that the attack is being guided from there."

Lowie roared a suggestion. "Oh dear," Em Teedee said. "Master Lowbacca suggests we would be well advised to go to the heart of the problem and leave these well-trained Wookiee gunners to continue the fight here. I agree that it might be safer to go inside—but I am skeptical about the wisdom of rushing into greater danger."

"Good idea, Lowie," Jacen said, ignoring Em Teedee's warnings. He fired the quad-laser one more time, almost off-handedly, and was astonished to see his quick shot destroy the side panel of another TIE fighter, which spun out of control to explode into the treetops. "Hey, got another one," he said.

"Let us go," Tenel Ka said. "If Imperials control the command center, we must hurry."

Inside the barricaded traffic control tower, Zekk listened to the outraged Wookiees outside pounding against the sealed door. A sizzling, melting sound worked its way into the background din as the Wookiees used high-intensity laser torches to slice through the armored metal. But Kashyyyk's own well-constructed defenses worked against them, since they had intended their command center to be impregnable. Slowly but surely, however, the Wookiees made headway, slicing through the door one centimeter at a time.

Using the security monitors, Zekk watched the

Wookiees out in the hall. With bestial rage one of the hairy creatures picked up a metal pipe and hammered at the door—to no effect, of course, because of the thick plating. But the Wookiee seemed satisfied to vent his fury.

Tamith Kai crossed her arms over her reptile-armored chest, scowling. "The noise level out there is most annoying," she said, then glared at the lone stormtrooper standing guard just inside the doorway. Her violet eyes flashed with a twisted idea. "Why don't we trigger the locking mechanism, let the Wookiees stumble inside, then take care of the whole lot before they recover from their surprise?"

Vonnda Ra chuckled. "That would be amusing to watch."

Before Zekk could voice an indignant protest that *he* was in command of this mission, not the looming Nightsisters, the stormtrooper activated the door controls. The armor plating suddenly slid aside, shocking the Wookiee engineers who had been working so intently to gain access. They howled.

The stormtrooper used his blaster rifle to mow them down in a few seconds, every one of them. Even encased in white armor, the stormtrooper's body language showed his pleasure. He keyed in the sequence again to slam the heavy door shut again, leaving the fallen Wookiees out in the corridor.

"At last, peace and quiet," Tamith Kai said.

Overhead the TIE fighters and bombers continued their attack, dodging bursts of weapons fire from the tree facility's perimeter defenses. Through the reinforced dome, they could see the battle in the skies. But they had no immediate idea of the rest of the struggles.

Several contingents of stormtrooper reinforcements already should have landed, however.

Vonnda Ra worked at one of the computer stations, scanning security monitoring images. A minute later, she gave a gasp of surprised triumph. "Ah, I believe I've found them," she said. "The vermin were apparently firing the perimeter guns, but now they're in the corridors. They seem to be making their way . . . ah! It seems they're making their way here. Delusions of grandeur. That could prove quite convenient."

"Who?" Zekk said.

Vonnda Ra raised her eyebrows. "Why, those Jedi brats, of course. Most of them, anyway. Had you forgotten your other goal for this mission?"

Zekk thought of Jacen and Jaina and their friends. "No, I haven't forgotten," he said. But he didn't want to confront the twins here, not in front of Tamith Kai. "We'll meet them on the way. Ambush them. Lock down their location."

"Simple enough," Vonnda Ra said.

Reinforcing his position of command, Zekk turned sharply and issued brisk orders. "Tamith Kai, you will remain here and continue organizing the mission. Our primary goal is to get those computers for the Second Imperium. You—" he nodded toward the stormtrooper "—will stay here as guard. Vonnda Ra and I will take care of the young Jedi Knights."

Tamith Kai scowled at being ordered about, but Zekk rounded on her, his black cape swirling. "Is that assignment beyond your capabilities, Tamith Kai?"

"Indeed not," she said. "Is yours? Just be certain you eliminate those brats."

When the stormtrooper unsealed the armored door again, Vonnda Ra followed Zekk as they strode out into the corridors, stepping around motionless Wookiee engineers sprawled on the floor, heading toward the confrontation with his former friends.

Jacen rushed along, shoulder-to-shoulder with Lowie and Sirra. The interior corridors were full of smoke, sparks, and noise. The glowpanels in the ceilings flickered off and on as energy fluctuations from the attack took their toll.

Tenel Ka had picked up a loose metal rod, a piece of destroyed pipe that had toppled from an overhead assembly. She loped along behind them, guarding the rear, holding the metal rod like a spear, as if hoping to find some enemy target.

Lowie and Sirra turned the corner in the corridor, and Jacen now thought he recognized the route they had taken to the monolithic control tower during their peaceful visit with the Tour Droid. Suddenly, Lowie gave a surprised roar; Sirra bellowed in alarm. Tenel Ka brandished her long metal rod.

"It's Zekk!" Jacen shouted, skidding to a stop.

There in the corridor, waiting for them, stood the dark-haired scamp who for years had been a friend to Jacen and Jaina . . . who had taken them on countless excursions to Coruscant's abandoned building levels and dim subterranean alleys. Now the once-scruffy boy wore expensive leather armor and a scarlet-lined black cape.

Tenel Ka saw Zekk, too, and held her metal staff at the ready. In a flash of memory, Jacen thought of the warrior girl's initial meeting with Zekk: The young man had dropped down from above to surprise them, but with blurring speed Tenel Ka had whipped out her fibercord and lassoed Zekk before he could jump out of the way.

Now, though, Tenel Ka had only one hand, and she did not choose to drop her long steel rod to grab for her rope.

For a moment Zekk's face seemed to open. His eyes grew round and surprised, uncertain. "Jacen," he said. "I—"

Then the muscular Nightsister beside him held up her clawlike hands. "There you are, Jedi brats!" she said.

Jacen could feel dark power crackling through the air. Fire-blue lightning bolts danced at the Nightsister's fingertips, burning through her body and sizzling behind her eyes as she raised her fingers. "I'll enjoy destroying you."

She flicked her wrists, ready to hurl her dark lightning at them—but Zekk shouldered the Nightsister to one side. The deadly bolts of evil force flared past them like shadowy flames that scorched a dark sinuous stain on the facility wall plates.

The Nightsister turned to glare at Zekk, but he snapped, "They are for me to deal with! *I* am in command here."

"I have your name, Vonnda Ra," Tenel Ka said in a low, threatening voice. "I saw you try to lure others from the Singing Mountain Clan on Dathomir. In your encampment at the Great Canyon I convinced you to choose me as a trainee for the Shadow Academy, but instead we rescued my friends—and defeated you utterly. We'll defeat you again."

With a thundering sound of booted feet, a contingent of stormtroopers charged down the corridor behind Zekk and Vonnda Ra. Jacen looked up with alarm. More reinforcements had arrived.

White-armored fighters must have landed on the upper platforms. The Second Imperium wanted something here at the fabrication facility. Judging from the alarms and explosions, the Imperials had already overrun the platforms.

Zekk stood waiting to battle the young Jedi trainees, as if gathering up his courage and his anger, while the rebuffed Nightsisters seethed with their own dark energy beside him. The stormtroopers drew their weapons.

Jacen knew with sudden certainty that they could never win the face-to-face fight here. Tenel Ka pushed herself one step forward, brandishing her metal rod. "We must turn back," she said, glancing over her shoulder at him.

"Good idea," Jacen said, casting a glimpse behind him.

"You, girl, are a traitor to Dathomir!" Vonnda Ra spat, just as Tenel Ka hurled the long pipe in her direction. The rod struck the Nightsister, knocking her sideways. Stormtroopers clattered toward them as Lowie and Sirra turned to charge back down the corridor.

"After them!" Zekk called, gesturing with one black-gloved hand.

The stormtroopers thundered in pursuit. Vonnda Ra cast the pipe aside. Patches of it were bent and red-hot, where fire from within the Nightsister's fingers had damaged the metal.

Sirra yelled something to her brother as they sprinted down the corridor, with Jacen and Tenel Ka right behind them. "Access hatch?" Em Teedee translated.

"Escape? Yes, that sounds like an excellent idea. By all means, let us escape."

At an intersection of corridors, Sirra stopped beside a clearly marked floor panel. Reaching down, she hooked the tiny ring-handles. With her powerful muscles, she hauled upward, pulling the heavy access hatch free to reveal a hole in the floor: a trapdoor. She growled and gestured.

Without hesitation Lowie leaped into the hole, catching a strong vine that hung underneath. The tinny voice of the translating droid wailed, "But this leads to the underlevels of the forest! Perilous and uncivilized. Master Lowbacca, we *can't* go down here. It's far too dangerous!"

Lowie merely grumbled and continued his descent. Tenel Ka followed next, hopping lightly over the edge, and wrapping her muscular legs around a vine. Grasping it with her hand, she rapidly lowered herself into the darkness.

Jacen turned around just in time to see Zekk and Vonnda Ra rushing toward them, flanked by storm-troopers. "Down into the underworld, huh?" Jacen said, glancing at Sirrakuk. "Looks like you'll get an early chance to perform that initiation rite of yours."

Sirra growled her agreement. With that, both of them plunged over the lip of the trapdoor and descended into the murky, leafy depths below.

Scrambling downward into the thick, tangled underbrush, Jacen looked up through the dense branches to see the silhouetted figures of Zekk and Vonnda Ra at the edge of the glowing patch of light. Jacen could hear their voices faintly as the group of young fugitives fled deeper into the thick forest.

"We'll have to follow them," Zekk said.

"You should have allowed me to destroy them when I had the chance," the Nightsister snapped. "Now they will cause difficulties."

Zekk answered sharply. "*I* am in charge here. We'll do things my way." He turned and shouted to the stormtroopers. "Down into the forests. All of you."

Zekk, Vonnda Ra, and the group of stormtroopers plunged after their prey into the underworld of Kashyyyk.